For family, near and far

In an interview some time later, Lillian remembered:

"The telephone rang, waking me on the third or fourth ring. My
caller

i. d. read, 'San Juan', but it was not my father's phone number. "

One: Lillian

Her brothers were calling her. Each had found what they had come for and it was getting late. Their flight from Newark to San Juan was due to take off in less than three hours. Kissing and hugging their mother goodbye, the three Levi children climbed into the rented Jeep Renegade departing as suddenly as they had arrived.

As they pulled on to the main road, Lillian looked back at the house until it was out of view. How long had it actually been since she sunbathed in the back yard while her father gardened, music streaming from the radio? She would change the station from oldies to hip-hop as soon as he was out of earshot, yet when she woke from her lazy tanning trance to apply more lotion, there it was again: the strains of one of her father's favorite songs:

"Though we've got to say good-bye for the summer, darling, I promise you this: I'll send you all my love, every day in a letter, and seal it with a kiss."

The traffic on the way to the airport was surprisingly light. Jack, Dashell and Lillian Levi arrived at Newark Liberty Airport thirty minutes before boarding time. It was Wednesday, March 19, 2008.

1

Lillian had made all the arrangements for the flights and the hotel. She could not leave important details to either of her brothers. This trip was mainly her idea anyway. She missed her dad. Maybe she missed the way things used to be. Whatever; she needed a break.

Jack was the only one of the three who would be checking luggage. He decided at the last minute to bring the personal items he gathered at his mom's home to Colorado. "You two go ahead . . . I will meet you around here as soon as I'm finished." He pointed to a delicatessen along the corridor. "I want to check this stuff."

"You're always ordering us around," Lillian shot back as she and Dashell picked up their carry-ons and walked to the deli.

"Well, I am not going to wait for Gunga Din's return to order a sandwich that's for sure. I'm starving." Dashell feigned an exaggerated starvation collapse in the center of the corridor. Scowling passengers whizzed past this playful spectacle. Weaving at the last moment, one elderly traveler sidestepped, cursed and stared in a single graceful movement defying her age.

"Wait until we get on the plane before you eat anything, you." Lillian was laughing as she grabbed his arm with her free hand so that her brother could stand and regain his balance. "The airline food won't be any better or worse, and we're boarding in ten minutes. We haven't even gone through security yet."

"Ok, but no cocktail peanuts for me!"

"It's a deal!" Lillian pumped the self-service coffee from the carafe into her cup. Shaking a sugar packet twice, she was already looking

2

forward to returning home, to the ordered life she now lived; her job, new town and pets. After accepting the teaching position at the County Day School, Lillian felt settled. It wasn't her dream-job, but it was something. Now reaching for the tiny *pour-shun* creamer, Lillian gazed through the coffee shop windows, past the airport parking lots, toward the Watchung Mountains.

"Lillian, you two decide between the middle seat and the window. I'm taking the aisle."

"You always have to be the boss, is that it, Jack?" Lillian jabbed him with her rolled up magazine, taking the window as Dashell squeezed in next. Earphones on, Jack was already in some other zone hearing nothing more during the entire San Juan flight.

She gazed out the window to the tarmac below where workers and tractors were moving about luggage, food storage containers, and packages of assorted sizes.

"Dashell, are Dad's books in the overhead?"

"Yeah, they're in my carry-on. Do you want them now?"

"Yes, please. I'm glad we brought them. I want Dad to have them."

Dashell reached around Jack and into the overhead compartment. Jack shoved him without looking up, and Dashell shoved him back. Opening the zippered carry-on without pulling it down, he made an attempt to remove the books bound together by elastic bands. Two well-worn journals, a loose-leaf notebook, hand-written notes on paper napkins, diner placemats and gum wrappers rained down like confetti. Most of the passengers in their section had not yet boarded, so picking

3

up the books and debris from the isle and under the seats was mercifully quick.

Dashell tossed the pile past Jack and into Lillian's lap. Flipping through one of the journals, Lillian exposed photographs and drawings to the first light of day in at least two years. Most likely these journals had been unused for longer than that. In fact, Lillian couldn't remember the last time her dad was around, not to mention make an entry in the journals that were now in her possession. She settled in to do some reading, but the boarding passengers and the busy flight crew were distractions that would not allow her to concentrate.

Shortly into the flight, Lillian sipped a diet coke and crunched some complimentary peanuts from the attendant. "My brother might not like these, but I do," she thought smugly, popping them into her mouth two at a time. Tilting her seat back slightly, she opened one of the journals at random and leafed through the hand-written notes. Her father's writing followed a pattern but Lillian had no idea what that pattern might be.

"Chronological?" she asked herself, elbowing Jack. "What is with all these flashbacks and leaps to the present?"

Jack removed one ear bud.

"You want me for something'?"

That was how it went for the flight. Lillian would alternately read and look out the window. In between journal pages she and Dashell would make small talk.

Lillian placed the journals in her carry-on bag before deplaning.

"Wow, Friday night in San Juan!" she cheered as the three travelers walked toward the main terminal. Lillian squeezed Dashell's arm but he pulled away quickly, not wanting to be babied. She retaliated by hurrying ahead of her brothers to the baggage area.

When Jack caught up, he suggested, "There's no need to rush. The baggage crew will take a while unloading my suitcase. Why don't we duck in here for a cool drink and figure out how we are going to get out of the airport?" pointing to the tacky theme restaurant, *Bar Tiki*. The place had an inviting island bar facade decorated in the colors and patterns of the Caribbean. There was even an artificial grass thatched roof and tall bamboo bar stools that ran the outside of the counter, the type that tourists expected in an island airport terminal.

"Latte for me, Jack please," Lillian replied promptly so that Jack would have to pay. They had played this cat and mouse game ever since she could remember; and it was Jack who had a trick up his sleeve that would cost her and Dashell their allowance as kids. Later, when they were working part-time, Jack's tactics would usually cost them a few dollars from their paychecks. They were always watchful of their brother's plans and schemes.

"Pepsi," Dashell added, smiling and picking up on his sister's quick reaction.

A drink later they were ready for action.

"Well, where do you suggest we go from here?" Dashell asked, looking toward his brother, accentuating the question by raising his eyebrows slightly.

"That depends on which rental company you called."

"National, I think," Dashell jugged his portable stereo from hand to hand, almost dropping it as he checked the rental car paperwork attached to his ticket.

"Yup, it's National."

"We're out of here. Guys, follow me!" Jack picked up his luggage and led the way to all the excitement that was lying just beyond Airport Drive and their rental car.

An hour later they arrived at the San Juan Hilton, which was not more than ten miles away.

"Next time, I will be in charge of the map," Jack proclaimed from the back seat as he grabbed it away from Dashell. Then he pulled the brim of his brother's baseball cap firmly down over his eyes. Dashell pushed his brother away and fixed the cap.

Lillian preened her hair a bit then swatted Jack as if he were an annoying insect.

"Dashell, thanks for reminding me to ask for adjoining rooms . . . a room for me and a room for the two of you, just as it should be.

"Thank you, sister dear, but I was hoping for the single. I know you wouldn't mind bunking with Jack."

"I don't think so." Lillian shook her head and laughed.

Lillian flashed back to a family vacation when she was a teenager. On holiday with her family in rural Pennsylvania, her brothers shared a motel room with their father, and Michael allowed her to have one of her own. Lillian's mother had to stay behind at the last moment due to a family illness. Looking back, her father's generosity made sense, given that a young girl just coming into womanhood needed her privacy. At the time, however, Lillian thought that her father was allowing her a special privilege, one that she held over her brothers for some time, whenever they teased her about being a girl.

Jack and Dashell were already out and about exploring the grounds of the hotel by the time Lillian knocked for them. She was eager to find her father. Obviously her brothers were more interested in finding the San Juan nightlife.

"No doubt they are checking out the pool, or one of the clubs off the main lobby," Lillian thought, planning her next move. She was unconcerned. Dashell had promised that if they got separated, he and Jack would return for her sooner or later so that they could all grab a late meal and listen to the Puerto Rican *Plenaro* Band featured on the hotel's restaurant marquee. That sounded great to Lillian, who was fond of seafood as well as an occasional drink with rum and coconut, even if she could never remember the name. Still she wanted to set out to find her father. When she had tried calling his cell phone, there was no answer.

Her father had written about the enticing island drinks in last year's birthday card.

" . . . Lillian, try to get here sometime soon. The boat drinks will float you away . . . hurry . . . miss you." Love, Dad

"I might indulge tonight before setting out in the morning to find you, Father dear. Thanks for the suggestion," Lillian said aloud, setting his journals neatly aside. While unpacking the few things she brought, Lillian sang softly to herself. Carrying the tune to the shower, the hot water and abundance of soapsuds washed the tensions of the day down the drain.

Wrapped in a towel, she rested on a bed that was much too large, even for two people. Later she would change into a comfortable evening outfit and sandals but for now, she felt her mind coming in for the landing her body had participated in hours before. Picking up one of the journals, she opened it to the makeshift airline napkin bookmark. She was beginning to relax.

"Who is it?"

"Hey, open up, you. Wait until you see what Jack got into!"

"Just a minute . . . must have fallen asleep. Can't you boys stay out of trouble?"

Jack was standing there in some sort of conquistador's helmet, looking ridiculous as usual.

"I am not going out with you looking like Cortez," Lillian emphasized closing the door on her brother, but Dashell had already pushed his way inside.

"Don't worry, Lillian, I'll leave it in the room . . . promise. Let's hit the hotel bar and turn this place up side down!"

"Ok, guys, but I'm coming back in a few hours."

Lillian turned away from them to close her door, but it slammed shut under its own power.

"Hey, one of you guys call Mom. Let her know that we arrived. Make reservations for lunch tomorrow at that place where dad hangs out. Ask the desk clerk the phone number and address. And another thing you better return that rental car. It will cost us a fortune to park every time we go out. We can just as well walk around here, or catch a taxi."

Lillian checked to see if her brothers heard all of her instructions, but they were already down the hallway and around the corner, making their way through the crowded lobby to the bar and restaurant adjacent to the pool area. With little need for doors and windows in this tropical climate, there seemed little difference between the inside and outside areas of the hotel. Lobbies and coffee bars flowed into breezy lounges that wound through lush plantings that lead to sparkling pools.

"Hey, wait up, guys." They were already out of sight.

Thursday, March 20

Awake before dawn and dressed in cutoffs and halter-top, Lillian made her way to the cozy coffee bar in the lobby.

"Night and day people . . . a world apart," Lillian said to herself. A young boy walked toward Lillian and stood just in front of her almost hidden by her newspaper. She lowered it slowly peeking just over the top to find him staring at her.

"Well, *hola*. What's your name?"

"Sean."

"Sean, where are your parents?"

The boy pointed toward the restaurant as his mother emerged. "Sean, don't bother that woman. Get over here."

"You had better get going, Sean," Lillian encouraged.

The boy ran to his mother without saying goodbye.

"Hey, sis, save some coffee for me," Dashell said. Her brothers approached from behind.

"What are you two doing up, or are you on your way to bed?"

"Who's your boyfriend?" Jack asked. "What seems to be the problem, sis', can't keep a real man around?"

"That is *so* funny . . . I'm picky, that's all."

"Right . . . hey, we haven't got all day. Let's blow this popsicle stand."

"Ok, let me go back to the room and get a few things. I'll meet you two out front in two minutes.

Away from the hotel portico and across the parking area, the Levi kids stretched their legs and welcomed the early San Juan sunshine.

"Hey, look . . . Iguanas!" Dashell shouted. Lizards of all sizes darted across their path, making a run for the waiting agaves in the chaparral beyond the pavement, the "Iguana Promised Land". The trio crossed the busy side street and walked toward a restaurant suggested by the concierge.

Dos huevos con café, $. 99 the sign in the window advertised.

"Is that price in dollars or pesos, Jack?"

"Cents, I think."

"Right within my budget," Lillian smiled and tugged on Jack's arm. "Let's eat!" They chose a small table by the window. After waiting a few minutes Jack became impatient.

"Maybe you should go over there and order, brother," Lillian smiled and pointed to a window where a woman was writing something on an unseen pad. Behind her, dishes clattered and people shouted.

As Jack approached the counter he turned to Lillian and Dashell. "What do you two want?"

"Eggs, potatoes, toast, coffee," she replied.

"Same," Dashell added.

"Make it three then . . . huevos, papas, uh, toast, café, por favor,"

"*Ciertamente. Tomar asiento y me lo traera a usted ed immediate*," the woman replied, motioning in the direction from where he Jack had come. The breakfast arrived within five minutes, the coffee was hot, and everything tasted delicious.

"Let's walk this off," Dashell suggested.

"Great idea . . . now can we go see about Dad?" They paid the tab and walked a few blocks, ducking in and out of curio shops, lottery kiosks, and open air *Mercado's*.

"So Lillian, where's this place Dad hangs out, anyway? I don't even know where he lives," Dashell asked.

"I'm not sure of either answer, and I forgot to bring the information. I'll have to go back."

"Not me . . . you're on your own. I'm going down by the water. 'What do you say', Dash?"

Jack and Dashell continued walking toward the water's edge to Historic Old San Juan. Disappointed, Lillian returned to her hotel room. She placed a call to her father's phone, but couldn't remember if she was calling his home or cell phone. He didn't answer. She then called *Moorings*, but got an answering machine, announcing the restaurant's hours of business and their menu.

Lillian changed into her bathing suit and headed poolside to read more of her father's journals. Sipping a pina colada from a tray of sample shots the waitress had brought to her, she stretched out on an available chaise lounge. The weather was beautiful, with large billowing clouds floating by almost for the touch. Her eyes were drawn to the blue-green hues of the Caribbean Sea and Atlantic Ocean, as they merged off the shores of San Juan, creating an artist's pallet of color.

So soothing were the gentle breezes that came across the pool, caressing Lillian's meticulously moisturized cheeks, that she decided to savor these moments and allow her mind to drift as it would, carried aloft by the balmy trade winds. It was not long before she gave in to dreams:

Her father was there, not smiling, she was sure . . . her mother was there, no . . . another woman . . . someone else . . . water . . .

Waking after what seemed like a short nap, the visiting sun was already a memory to a darkened sky. "I couldn't have slept the whole day away," Lillian wondered as she stood up from her chaise lounge folded her towel, grabbed the journals and headed toward her room. A sudden gust of wind blew open one of the journals, sending scraps of notes flying toward the pool.

"Damn," Lillian shouted, scurrying after the loose bits, catching the last of them before they reached the water. Lillian looked upward . . . dark clouds were forming; low, thick and threatening. Pulling her hair back with her right hand and clutching her possessions she fled to the sheltered staircase and hallways leading to her room, her hot shower and her Caribbean evening.

Lillian knocked on the adjoining door. No answer. They would have to be in one of the hotel's restaurants, at the poolside tiki bar, or walking the beach. She had hoped that she and her brothers would make their way to *Moorings* that evening, but she had slept the afternoon away, her brothers were nowhere to be found, and there was no message from her father. After her shower, she put on a light sundress, taking care to apply soothing cream to areas that she had missed with her suntan lotion.

"Oohh," she moaned, touching her tender shoulders. I'll be more careful tomorrow."

Jack and Dashell finally showed up a little after seven pm. "Well, where have you guys been?" she asked, her hands on her hips.

"Sorry Lil," Dashell returned, apologetically. It's one of the mysteries of the Caribbean . . . how the time just passes."

"That's right . . . sorry, Lillian," Jack added, his key card passing through the beam of light that allowed the door to unlock. Shedding clothes, Jack ran for the shower. "I claim firsts," he called over his shoulder.

"How old are you guys, anyway?" Lillian called after them, but she should have known better than to ask. The water was already on. Dashell threw Lillian a guilty look and shrugged. She shook her head from side to side and returned to her room where she plopped on the bed, grabbed the remote and waited for her brothers.

Worn out from their walking tour and full of excuses, the boys convinced their sister to dine at the hotel rather than venture into town once more. They promised to take her to Moorings for lunch the following day. "If Dad were in San Juan, we would have run into him by now," Dashell said, his hand on Lillian's shoulder. Disappointed, Lillian glanced at the menu on the desk and pondered the pros and cons of seafood over steak.

Friday, March 21

"You have got to be kidding." The hand-written sign in the window listing the hours of operation read that it would be open, today only, at 6 pm.

"What time is it now?"

"It's only a little after ten, sis." Only Lillian seemed discouraged, and again the boys wanted to take off for site seeing. Lillian was not eager to join them.

"C'mon, Lil, don't be a spoil sport. We didn't see you all day yesterday, right Jack?"

Jack was tight-lipped.

"Jack?" Dashell asked again, rolling his eyes from his brother to his sister, nudging his brother to answer.

"Right, Brother . . . Lillian, Join us."

Lillian gave in, and they headed off together for the day's events.

Early that evening, Lillian walked to *Moorings Bar and Grill*, by herself this time. She would not be talked out of her mission. Her brothers already had made dates with the two college girls who were spending the weekend at the hotel with one of the girls' parents. The young woman had come to the Hilton with her family and brought along her girlfriend for company. What a stroke of luck for the Levi brothers.

"You go, Lillian, and let us know how you make out. Call or text us if you find Dad, and we can meet up then," Jack said.

"Look at it this way, Lil. If Dad were in San Juan he would have made contact," Dashell added. "Doesn't that make sense? He must've left for his vacation already."

"Ok, then, catch you two later." She kissed each of her brothers on the cheek, and slapped Jack on the butt. "Stay out of trouble, and keep an eye on your baby brother."

Lillian entered the bar and allowed her eyesight to adjust to the dark atmosphere. A band was playing bluegrass music from the small stage in the dining room. Lillian was looking for Denis Gutierrez Rodriguez, the owner of the restaurant. Her father said Denis would have a package for her if he were not in San Juan to meet her.

"Sir, is Mr. Rodriguez here?"

"One minute, Miss. I'll get him." A few minutes later the bartender returned with another man.

"So you must be Lillian."

Lillian nodded and accepted his hand. "Yes, how'd you guess?"

"You're just as your father described you . . . and your father showed me a picture," he added, a grin breaking on his face. "I came by before. The sign said."

"Yes . . . sorry . . . I was called away to an appointment . . . your father told me to expect you this weekend, so you are right on schedule, see? Welcome to Puerto Rico. Please, have a cold drink."

"Beer, thank you."

Denis motioned to the bar. "So then my father is already off to Mexico?"

"Yes, I'm afraid so. He did leave something for you, though. Let me get it. I'll be just a minute." Denis excused himself and disappeared through a pair of swinging doors. Lillian stepped up to the bar and accepted a draft beer from the barmaid, and as a foam mustache bubbled on her upper lip, she took in her surroundings. Denis returned with a manila envelope for Lillian. Undoing the clasp, she reached in and removed the contents: a journal with a sticky note attached with the words, "For Lillian." She recognized the handwriting as her father's. Lillian thanked Denis for being so considerate as to keep an eye out for her, and invited him to join her in a drink. Keeping her mug of beer in her left hand and carrying the journal securely in her right, she followed her host as he made his way through the gathering of couples and singles to a nearby table. Lillian turned the leather-bound book in her hand, noticing for the first time the art on the cover. She recognized this particular journal as one her father purchased in San Antonio while they were on a family vacation when she was still in high school. On the River Walk, a trendy tourist area not far from the Alamo, her father purchased two journals from a local craftswoman; one for himself and one for her. Both journals were covered with animal hide and had leather ties. Lillian remembered making her first entry as she was having lunch that day. It was just after the gondola ride that took her family and a boatload of passengers on a slow journey down the secluded canal:

. . . as we slowly motored along the River Walk, our guide announced through his loudspeaker that, "more than 500 years ago when the Spanish Conquistadors landed in what is now Mexico, they encountered the indigenous peoples practicing a certain ritual . . . one where they appeared to be mocking death. These practices are observed and celebrated in modern times in early November here in Texas and all along the Mexican border. The Americans among us on our tour this morning will know this holiday as Halloween, All Hollow's Eve, or All Saints' Day." A teenage boy threw something in the water. A baby babbled, and then cried. I nodded my head in understanding as my father snapped a picture of me with the gondolier, our photographic record affirming what we were told about The Day of the Dead (El Dia di las Muertes).

Lillian felt proud when her father, looking over her shoulder in their room at the River Walk Hyatt that evening, told her, "You will certainly be a writer of note one day".

Leafing through a few more pages written and illustrated in her father's hand, Lillian placed the journal on the table. She turned to her host and with a smile inquired, "So, Denis, have you known my father for a long time?" the foam of her draft beer now drying just above her upper lip, her tongue attempting to discretely reach for every bit; "not ladylike," she thought, "but delicious."

Denis was quiet for a few moments as he studied his empty glass. "No, I can't say that I've known your father for very long; only a few months. On the other hand, it seems like I know him well. When your father comes to *Moorings*, he comes to have a nice dinner with us, to write, sometimes to talk."

"When did he leave San Juan?"

"He left a few weeks ago with a friend of his. I understand that his friend came back. Your father didn't."

"And why is that?"

"I don't know why he extended his stay. Perhaps he had business."

"That's kind of strange, no? Wasn't he supposed to come right back?"

"That was the plan, yes. I'm sure everything's all right." Denis called for a shot from the bar.

"Well, where is his friend . . . ?"

"Max."

"Max. Can I ask Max about my father?"

"You could, but I hear that he went back to the states to visit his daughter."

There was a silence on Lillian's part.

"Well, young lady, I've got to get back to work." Denis wished Lillian good luck in her journey to catch up with her father. Extending his hand he stood up and gazed at her longer than was the custom, leaving her to her thoughts as he walked away from the table. Denis then stopped and turned.

"Miss Levi, if you don't find your father in Cancun, then you might try Havana."

Thinking that Denis was making a joke, she walked over to him, gave him a hug, and thanked him again for all his help. Returning to her table, she lifted her mug in salute as he walked away. A final sip finished off her glass. The bartender sent another to her table.

Lillian turned and nodded. "No charge," he returned the nod, wiping his hands his dishtowel. Turning her attention to what she had come for, she found a piece of paper that belonged to one of her father's other journals. The velum of the paper was lighter in texture and of a different color than the one Denis had just given her. As she moved her index finger along the edge of the orphaned piece, Lillian recognized the texture as the type belonging to the journals she had brought to San Juan. The single page contained a poem, or a portion of one. From the torn sheet of paper, Lillian read:

The Man with the Butterfly Tattoo, and the Angel Who Loved Him

A man, longing for intimacy, met a woman whose entire being beckoned him, yet he did not know why.

"I am an angel," she told him, "and I have been looking for you."

"Take me with you to heaven, then," he replied.

"What would be the use of that?" the angel shrugged. "Angels do not know that they are in heaven. It is your human-ness that we seek."

At once the man's heart was opened, and ten thousand butterflies took flight and settled at the feet of the man and his angel, creating a soft bed. The two made such gentle and deliberate love as not to disturb any butterfly save one.

That one butterfly became a tattoo on the arm of the man so that if the lovers were ever separated in this world, the angel would be drawn by the pounding of the man's heart; NO! But for the desperate, furious beating of the wings of the man's painfully neglected butterfly tattoo.

The torn sheet of paper had been placed in the journal next to the page that held more poetry:

. . . And if the lovers were ever in the same stadium,
The same shopping mall, or the same church,
They never knew it, for
Their paths never crossed again.

Lillian placed the second poem between the pages of the first, and closed the journal.

"Depressing stuff, my father writes." Leaving a tip that covered more than the price of the free beer, she walked toward the exit. As she pushed the door open letting in the rush of street sights and sounds, Lillian heard Denis call her name from the other side of the bar:

"Miss Levi, one other thing . . ."

Jack and Dashell had been gone all afternoon.

"I must say brother that was a great swim." Jack whacked him with a rolled up towel as they approached the pool patio area.

"I must say to you too, brother, that she was a great lifeguard." Dashell returned the sting of his towel.

"There's Lillian . . ." Jack pointed to their sister's chaise. Dressed in her brand new bikini a drink in her hand and her father's journals in her lap, Lillian appeared content.

"Hey, Lil', look what Jack bought!" Dashell shouted, grabbing her drink and taking a sip.

Lillian lowered her sunglasses. "Hey, get your own drink, Dash." Turning her attention to Jack, yes he did look handsome in his straw hat and Hawaiian shirt. Exaggerations of tropical wear to be sure, but her brother would look good in anything.

"Let's get something to eat," Jack said. They're setting up the restaurant   for   dinner.

"Guys, tomorrow I'm going to Cancun. That's where Dad went."

"Yeah, right, like that's going to happen," Dashell replied.

"I'm serious. I'm going. You can come along if you wish."

"Come on, Lillian, leave Dad to his fun. You remember what it was like on your spring breaks. He probably is snuggling with some freshman right now. The last thing he will want is his family around.

"For your information I do remember spring break, and I didn't do any snuggling . . . not with men old enough to be my father anyway."

"Forget about going to Mexico."

Lillian still insisted that she was going to Cancun on Saturday and a swift wave of her hand indicated she would not be changing her mind.

Saturday, March 22

Lillian placed her father's writings along with her own into her carry-on and headed for the lobby where her brothers would be waiting. Stopping at the front desk she paid their collective balance on a credit card and asked the bell captain to arrange a ride to the airport.

"I may have taken a drink or two from the refrigerator in the room."

"No problem, miss, the first two are a courtesy."

Lillian was anxious to gather up her brothers and be on her way. There was no sign of them as she scanned the busy lobby, but familiar voices from the newspaper stand told her that they were not far away. She now had them in her sights. Jack was speaking with the cashier and Dashell then came into view. He was thumbing through a magazine. Lillian picked up her receipt and walked toward the sheltered exit where a taxi was already waiting, its engine running. Dashell saw her and followed.

"Jack will be here in a sec. You know how he is."

Lillian handed a piece of paper to the driver as he opened the trunk for their luggage. He nodded to her indicating that he knew the address.

"I call shotgun," Dashell shouted.

"Sorry, pal, already there," Jack shot back as he made a run for the front passenger's door. He was in the seat with the door closed, his luggage on his lap, before his brother could give chase. "Some things never change," Lillian whispered, shaking her head as she climbed into the rear, behind the driver's seat.

The note that Lillian handed the driver was the same one she found among the pages of the journal Denis had given her. It contained her father's San Juan address, with a request that if he were not in San Juan to greet them, would they go to his home water his plants and open the windows a crack.

"What's the plan, Lil?" Jack asked, realizing they would not be traveling directly to the airport.

"I want to stop by Dad's condo. It's only a few minutes out of our way." Then, clutching the driver's seat she pulled herself forward and asked, "My father's home is on the way to the airport, isn't it, Senor?" The driver nodded. Soon he was guiding his cab to the curb in front of a small condominium complex.

"This is it, senorita," he turned and smiled, pointing to a cluster of housing beyond the sidewalk where he parked. "Better hurry . . . we still have a way to go."

"Thank you. We'll be right back."

The driver selected a CD from a small stack tucked in the console of his Toyota 4-door.

Lillian looked over her shoulder as she walked up the path toward the front steps. "Don't worry sister," Dashell whispered in her ear as they approached the front door. "He won't leave without his fare."

They did a quick walk-through: one bedroom, one bath, an eat-in kitchen, and a living room crowded with tropical plants and a computer. The bookshelf was neatly organized with textbooks, novels, and magazines. A daybed doubled as a sofa.

"How long has dad been here?" Jack asked.

"One semester, I think."

"Well, it didn't take him long to settle in. I have to use the bathroom."

"Dashell spotted a note on the wooden kitchen table, leaning against the napkin holder.

"Hey, Lil, check it out," he said, motioning in the direction of the note.

"Lillian, I'm sorry I missed you. I will be staying at the Hyatt Caribe in Cancun. Hope to see you there. A room will be waiting for you. The boys can bunk with me. Love, Dad."

Lillian folded the note and stuffed it in her rear jean pocket.

"Count me out, Lil," Dashell said, without removing his head from the refrigerator. "I have to be back at work on Monday."

"I can't go either . . . sorry, Lillian," Jack returned from the bathroom. "Why not leave Dad to his fun? Come home with us."

"No, it would be good to see him. I'm going,"

Jack shrugged. "Is there anything to eat in there, Dash?"

"Come on, guys, out of the fridge. We've got to get out of here." Taking a final survey of the neatly arranged apartment, Lillian watered her father's plants, and washed the single plate and cup in the sink, carefully placing the dishes in the drying rack. The windows were already open a crack, or she would have taken care of that too.

"We didn't get to see Dad, but at least we now know where he lives." Dashell broke the silence as the cab driver unloaded their bags. His eyebrows were raised in a peculiar expression of encouragement.

"That was something, anyway," Jack added. No one else was smiling except the driver and there was no telling what he was so happy about. He tapped his ring finger on the steering wheel as he popped in another compact disc. Soon he was taking their bags out of the trunk curbside at the airline terminal. Immediately after Lillian paid the fare and tip, the driver sped away.

"Come here, guys. Give me a big hug. Wish me luck!" Dashell was the first to respond to her call for affection.

"Safe trip, Lil," Jack said, "and make sure you tell Dad we told you not to follow him."

"Don't be such a sore loser. You two want me all to yourselves." Hugging and kissing good bye, each in turn picked up a piece of luggage and headed for their respective gates, promising to get in touch the following weekend.

It was late Saturday afternoon by the time Lillian descended the wheeled stairway and stepped onto the tarmac of Cancun International Airport. The westward wind and the low temperatures were just two of the surprises Lillian would receive on this afternoon. In the short time that she was in the Caribbean, she had acclimated to the warm sunshine and balmy weather, but here in Mexico something was different. The air was cooler and dryer.

An airport bus transported her and other passengers to Customs and Immigration. Lillian passed through this area with ease. Her passport was new with empty pages begging for customs stamps of romantic ports-of-call. Paperwork in order, she brought nothing that required declaration. Making her way along the main concourse and following the exit signs, she heard her name being paged over the address system asking her to report to the Information Counter.

"Hi, I'm Lillian Levi. Someone paged me?"

The agent handed her a telegram:

Lillian: I am at the Hotel Tejadillo in Havana, Cuba. Don't be mad. When you are rested join me. Love, Dad

"Fine," Lillian thought, slinging a bag over her shoulder . She had already made up her mind that she would find her father, and as she learned from her conversation with Denis her destination might very well turn out to be Cuba, but she still could not believe it. She thought of her conversation that night at Moorings:

"Miss Levi, one other thing..."

Turning and letting the door slam, she walked back to where Denis was standing.

"Yes?"

"Lillian, it would be a good idea for you to go after your father," Denis suggested in a controlled tone. *"Between you and me,"* drawing in closer, *"Your father has not been well, and may be in need of a good talking to and looking after."*

"I'm not sure I understand where this is going."

"Your dad asked me before he left San Juan not to share this information with anyone, but you are not just anyone."

"What are you talking about, Denis? Is my father dying or something? What exactly is the matter with him?"

"What I've just told you is all I know, Lillian. I think it would be better if you find out more for yourself. And please, if you do learn more, then you can share it with me, ok?"

"I absolutely will, Denis, and thank you."

"Good. Now be on your way. You will want to make connections for . . . Mexico."

"Miss, is there anything else I can do for you?"

"What?"

"The telegram, miss, do you wish to send a reply?"

"No, no thank you." Lillian folded the message and placed it back in the envelope. She stepped away from the information booth.

"Oh, this is just great," Lillian shouted, startling an elderly couple standing next to her at the information desk. Dressed in identical white sweat pants, sweat jackets, and baseball hats, the couple looked up at Lillian in unison, and without averting their eyes, cautiously

29

backed away. She was too tired to make any more decisions today. Sunday would be time enough to pack up and pick up. If it were true that her father had moved on to Cuba, she'd be on the next flight. Since there was a room reserved for a one-night layover in Cancun, she decided to rest.

Reading the signs over the ticketing desks in the Main Terminal of the airport, Lillian gained her travel bearings. She walked to the *Mexicali Airlines* information window and purchased a ticket to Havana for the following day, Easter Sunday. The agent gave her a choice of two flights that departed Cancun for Havana seven days a week. There was a mid-morning flight and another in the late afternoon. Lillian chose the earlier flight.

"It would be better to fly out in the morning, don't you think?" she asked the woman working the counter, seeking encouragement from this stranger. "Just in case I run into any problems, it'd be better to work them out in the daylight." The woman looked up, smiled, and continued processing the ticket. The cost of a round trip ticket was three hundred dollars, with additional service charges and taxes of course, and an additional fifty-dollar charge for the visa to enter Cuba. Lillian booked her return flight for the following Friday. If that departure date did not work out, she would worry about it later.

The time had come to change money. Lillian studied the rates on the *cambio* monetary exchange chart from American dollars to *pesos*, and American dollars to *euros*.

"No matter which currency you choose you will have to change to the Cuban peso when you arrive in Havana, senorita."

"Is one better than the other?"

"Pesos or euros, makes no difference. As long as the money is not American, you will be ok." Lillian changed most of her money into pesos then changed one hundred dollars into Euros, just to see which currency would take her the farthest.

"Is there a limit to what I can bring with me?"

"If you stay under five thousand dollars, there is no paperwork and few questions."

Clutching her passport in her right hand and with her single piece of luggage securely slung over her left shoulder, Lillian stepped through the exit doors and walked to the taxi stand. Hordes of anxious vacationers were moving about, hailing the taxicabs and hotel courtesy buses.

Within moments Lillian was tapped on the shoulder by a sky captain. "Would you like a taxi, senorita?" Soon she was holding on tightly to the door handle as her cab zoomed out of the airport drive. The vehicle seemed to Lillian too old and flimsy to be traveling as fast as it was now daring to go, and she touched her neck as if to finger a religious piece of jewelry, the way she had seen women do in times of distress; a piece of jewelry that was not there but probably should have been.

The Hyatt Cancun Caribe' was located in a row of dozens of hotels that were turned out in cookie-cutter fashion on Cancun's scenic but overdeveloped tourist area just off shore from Laguna Nichunte', the protected body of water lying between the sand bar and the mainland. Lillian's father had recommended this Hyatt to her on more than one occasion during their conversations and emails, and since he was the one making and paying for the reservation, Lillian would take full advantage of his generosity.

"Levi," Lillian announced as she approached the check-in desk. The concierge processed her information, taking her credit card and issuing Lillian a door keycard, along with a small packet containing information about the Hyatt's features. The concierge then handed Lillian a note that was waiting for her in her mailbox.

"Don't tell me," Lillian said. "It's a note from Michael Levi, right?"

The woman said nothing but stood by, waiting for further instructions from Lillian:

"Lillian, if you have come this far, and if you wouldn't mind, would you please bring additional money with you to Havana? We may need it!   Love, Dad"

"Oh, brother . . . how good of you to include me in your financial planning." She folded the telegram and turned it over in her hand. By the time Lillian made it to Havana, her father would need as much money as Lillian could bring to him. "Who knows how much he will have left when I get there?"

"Excuse me?" the concierge leaned in as if she misheard.

"Nothing . . . thank you for the note. Where is the nearest bar?"

"We have three on site if you count the tiki bar." The concierge took a house brochure from the clear Lucite counter display, turned it over, and pointed to the map of the hotel and grounds. There's also the refrigerator in your room. I'll give you a key."

"Thanks. Do you know where I can get my hands on some money? I mean, if I were to leave here to travel . . . ?"

"Excuse me one moment, Ms. Levi." The woman left for a moment, returning just as quickly with a small canvas currency bag. "Mr. Levi, asked us to give this to you if you asked for it. Sign here and it's yours."

Lillian would carry $4,950 to her father, taken from the bag. The remaining money, nearly $550, she would ask the hotel to hold until she returned. On this vacation with little cash for herself, she preferred to use her credit cards.

So that was that. It was now time for a little shopping. "What a shame it would be to come all this way and not purchase a trinket or two-and now with all this cash." Before heading to her room, Lillian browsed in the trendy *Gift Shop*. She priced bathing suits in *The Beach Shop*. She drank a latte in *Ye Olde Bagel Shoppe*, and tried on sunglasses in *Eyewear*. Returning to *The Beach Shop* Lillian took another look at the bathing suits and naturally she needed to purchase suntan oils, which she left behind in San Juan. "I guess I take after mom," Lillian thought as she tossed her hair back in the way women do.

A hand-full of designer packages swinging from her arm, it was time to check out the room and shower before dinner. Tearing herself away from the boutiques that lined the hotel lobby, Lillian turned every man's head as she approached the bank of elevators. Slim, adorable and dark, but with an athletic build all but disguised with a fashionable wardrobe, Lillian gave the impression that she was somehow vulnerable. Nothing could have been further than the truth. She never stopped to evaluate herself beyond a look in the mirror, but if she took inventory, she would agree that she was "built to last", not unlike the way her father described an old English motorcycle he was tricked into buying one year with his tax return.

As the door closed and the elevator silently rose to the second floor; Lillian recalled part of her phone conversation with her father:

"Don't worry, Lillian. You'll have no trouble finding me in Mexico . . ."

"Right, Dad," she said aloud, running the hot water, testing it with a toe.

Lillian changed her clothes and dined at "O", the hotel's main restaurant. It featured buffet-style dining, with color-coding to help patrons choose their meals by caloric and nutritional guidelines. Once back in her room, she took a quick inventory of the clothing items she brought. She reached for her journal and threw herself on the firm, king-size bed:

"Only anxious lovers have messy rooms . . . Winding pathways guide these lovers through dune and landscape adjacent to the intruding surf . . . Broken conch shells are abundantly scattered by the previous high tide, "like so many broken tropical hearts, for others to gather" (where did I hear that . . . from a dream, perhaps?). The constant wind is not content to simply weave my hair into a hopeless tangle . . . It forces the clouds to travel from east to west too quickly for me to narrate the dragon stories that the billows of vapor spin . . . then the evening rain brings mysterious rhythms to my dreams as the rain is apt to do . . . .

Closing her eyes, Lillian set her journal on the bed. Literary images fell away, replaced by clouds and airplanes, and the cry of a large bird. A woman appeared; a dark woman, slender build, hair blowing freely all about her, her arms stretched out, reaching toward her . . .

"Do I know you?"

"Do you?"

"I don't think I've ever met you."

"Well, you might."

Sunday, March 23, Easter

She had been in a deep sleep for hours. Walking to the sliding doors that led to her small balcony, she drew back and secured the heavy curtains. Pushing the sliding door open, Lillian experienced the full impact of the pre-sunrise Cancun morning. With a whoosh warm salty air rushed in the room. The sun had not yet emerged from beneath the ocean. Peacocks were screeching just as they had all night long, a design decision of inane ambiance. Below her balcony was a shimmering swimming pool, shaped like a freeform pond with kidney-style coves for seclusion and main swimming areas for exercise. On the bridge connecting the two main swimming areas, Lillian made out the form of a man crossing over. Beyond the pool, the dark sea's roar seemed to beg for Lillian's company, the rhythmic lapping reaching for the edges of the sheltered swimming pool and cabana area.

She glanced at the alarm clock on her nightstand. It was a few minutes after six. She slipped her key card into her robe pocket and left the room, taking the nearest elevator down one flight to the main lobby.

Except for a short, heavy-set woman, dressed in white and operating a vacuum, the lobby was empty. A man, tall and formally dressed in the uniform of the day, was standing at the Concierge's Station. He was staring straight ahead, tapping a pencil slowly on his sign-in ledger. Discretely chewing gum, he nodded to Lillian as she walked by; his eyes following her like the black and white cat-eye clock in a grandma's kitchen.

Exiting the hotel through a central set of doors facing east, Lillian followed the walkway to the far end of the poolside patio area. Although not yet daylight, she could clearly make out the movement of the tide from her vantage point, shades of purple and black splattered against an even deeper sky, hinting at rain just off the coast.

A young, dark skinned man had been skimming the pool. Lillian stood watching him, her arms crossed as if she were embracing herself to keep warm. Her hair was now a mosaic of matted tangle as the movement of the air carried it behind her, toward the west. Lillian realized too late that it was a mistake not to have dressed before leaving her room. The pool boy turned to her. "*Mira*", he said calmly, pointing toward the ocean. As if at his command the dawn burst from the sea. As Lillian stood mesmerized, a flaming ball of light rose, drawing with it the light of a new day to this western Caribbean paradise. Nodding politely to acknowledge the young man's parlor trick, Lillian turned and faced the bridge that connected the pools. She saw again the man that she had glimpsed from her balcony, making his way back. Lillian turned and walked with long strides on the poolside walkways. She traveled up the path back toward the lobby entrance, retracing her steps from where she had come. Standing even with the bridge, Lillian noted that whoever was on the bridge, had moved on.

Approaching the doors that led back to the elevators, there was a tap on her shoulder. Lillian turned. It was the pool boy. Standing this close to him, she could see that he was in his late twenties, tan and muscular. She felt uncomfortable with him inside her comfort zone, and stepped back.

"*Lo siento, Senorita* . . . I'm sorry . . . will you be at the pool for breakfast?" If so, I can have a table set for you."

"Thank you. That would be great. Did you see anyone on the bridge a few moments ago?"

"No, Senorita."

"Can I sit near that bridge, maybe over there?" she asked, pointing to a table with an ocean and pool view.

"The table will be waiting for you. My name is Manuel. Look for me when you come to breakfast."

Returning to her room, Lillian put on her bathing suit. She decided to take a swim before breakfast. The air temperature was still cool from a balmy overnight, but the pool water had retained enough of the midday heat. She dove into the misty water. Skimming the bottom and blowing bubbles to keep her there, Lillian did the breaststroke and frog kick, imagining that she was a stingray gliding just above a sandy plain. The chlorine was too strong however, and she surfaced exhaling joyously and moving into a butterfly stroke splashing down with her chest sending pool water to the sidewalk beyond. That was enough for her. She showered, dressed and packed her few belongings. Leaving them with the Bell Captain, she placed her name on the list for a taxi to the airport.

"I will be ready to go in forty-five minutes."

"Very good, miss, your ride will be waiting right through those doors."

"Thank you. Do you have Internet?"

"Yes, down the hall and to the right."

"Thank you."

Lillian visited the Business Center to print out some general in formation about Havana. She also sent her mother an email:

Hi, Mom,

I am taking a few extra days to join dad. Talk to you soon.

Love, Lil . . .

She did not see Manuel but as Lillian approached the hostess stand, the hostess picked up a menu and escorted Lillian to a table near the swimming pool, within a few yards of the adjoining bridge. "The waiter will be here in a moment to take your order."

Manuel walked past her table just as she was removing a pit from her orange juice with her spoon. She looked, up, orange pulp telling the tale. Manuel asked her if she would like to join him for a drink that evening. Lillian thanked him and told him that she would be leaving Cancun for a few days, but hoped to return by the end of the week.

She did not mention where she was going. He told her that he would look for her.

The island of Cuba was visible beneath the clouds and to the northeast even before her aircraft was over the island. Arriving from the west and flying at an altitude of no more than 3000 feet above the Caribbean, Lillian could make out the lush vegetation of the coastal plain and the quilted farmland beyond. Ramshackle urban areas came into view as the airliner banked for its approach. Secondary roads and highways dotted with white structures of all shapes and sizes could be counted. Clearly visible now as her plane descended were automobiles and trucks, many of which were at rest, sitting idle in driveways, parking lots, front and back yards on the misty landscape. In sharp contrast to the regimented checkerboard landscape from higher altitudes, it was now apparent that many of the vehicles were inoperative, strewn about on rugged, neglected farmland, front lawns, and side streets.

The aircraft landed on that windy, unseasonably cold Easter Sunday, at 10:50am. Deplaning directly onto the tarmac from the rusty ladder that had been rolled up to the aircraft, Lillian slung her small overstuffed duffel over her shoulder and quickly boarded one of the three buses belching black exhaust fumes while waiting to take the new arrivals to the Immigration Terminal for processing. There was no guarantee Lillian would get past the immigration officers without a good story. Standing in line, she watched closely as each passenger's paperwork was examined for authenticity. Lillian was an American citizen traveling to the only communist country in the Western World; a communist country that was considered by her government an enemy of the United States, and she was traveling there without State Department approval.

Minutes ticked by as each traveler's papers were scrutinized. Finally it was Lillian's turn to present her credentials. She was summoned with a wave to the window by a young woman in a tailored and pressed uniform; a uniform worn in stark contrast to the carelessly dressed policemen standing by with guard dogs and antique Uzi weaponry, but not exactly poised for intercepting trouble. "Why have you come to Cuba, Miss?" the agent asked with a cadence in meticulously enunciated English.

"Tourist," Lillian replied, quickly averting her gaze. Her stomach dropped as she was asked to step aside for a moment. The woman motioned for another agent and a supervisor to come to her window. Lillian was sure her heart had stopped beating. The three government officials then summoned her back to the window.

"Welcome to Cuba." Then she handed Lillian her passport and visa.

In the taxicab Lillian, referring to a small softbound English-Spanish dictionary, asked the driver if he could suggest a hotel where she could find a room. She did not want to meet her father on the same day as her arrival, and wanted to rest overnight before making a fresh appearance. The taxi driver either misunderstood her or was being paid by a particular hotel to bring his fares there, because she was dropped off at a businessman's hotel in a run down industrial part of the city not far from the waterfront. This was not the Havana that Lillian had imagined when she did her Internet research in the morning hours leading up to her departure from Cancun.

By the time she checked into her room and had a moment to relax, it was 6 pm. Relieved that she would only have to wait a few hours before going to bed, she ate in the modest hotel restaurant, returning to her room with a cup of tea and a piece of cake. Securing the door with a bolt and chain that looked like as if it could be easily forced, she leaned the writing desk chair between her and the entry. Anyone trying to get to her would have do deal with that first. Under the covers by 9:30 pm, Lillian was sound asleep within minutes.

Her dreams were filled with pool boys and peacocks taking flight over multi-colored seas. Her brothers were there in comical poses, offering traveling advice. Her father was there too, on his hands and knees in his garden. He was saying something to her that she could not make out, although she strained to hear. She could not hear over the music scoring her dream:

" . . . *I'll see you, in the sunlight, hear your voice everywhere, I'll run to tenderly hold you, but darling you won't be there . . .*"

There was another woman in Lillian's dream, too; not herself, not her mother. The woman was handing something to her.

Monday, March 24

Splashing water on her face and applying a minimum amount of make-up, she dressed in jeans and pullover. She took the elevator down the two flights to the hotel lobby, where the concierge offered to arrange a taxi for her.

"Right this way, Senorita."

"No thank you. I will find my own way." Lillian picked up her bag and proceeded through the red and white striped awning walkway to the sidewalk.

"Senorita, it is not a good idea to venture out alone unescorted in Havana. Please, let me call you a taxi," the desk clerk pleaded as he held the door open.

"I'll be all right," she called over her shoulder.

The clerk shook his head, launched a cigarette into the front lawn of the hotel and closed the door.

Turning right, Lillian walked toward a stand of vehicles-for-hire parked caddy-corner at the next intersection. A number of young men were smoking cigarettes, drinking coffee and to Lillian it sounded like she interrupted a discussion about baseball.

"Gentlemen, do any of you know the Hotel Tejadillo?"

"Si, Senorita." A young driver no more than seventeen stepped forward and crushed his cigarette beneath his worn sneaker. He motioned for her to climb aboard his coco taxi. This was the curious yet efficient mode of urban transportation that Lillian had seen in a news program about Havana once. The wobbly vehicle was nothing more than a gas-powered motor scooter with an egg-shaped fiberglass body. It reminded her of something Mr. Magoo would drive. The molded rear section was designed to accommodate no more than two passengers, each with an indention for one small piece of luggage. Precarious yes, but for an adventurer like Lillian it would be a great way to see the city.

Seconds later driver and passenger were speeding along the *Malecon*, the scenic drive bordering the city waterfront.

The hotel was in the heart of *Habana Vieja,* the "old city". It was there Lillian came upon her father. Michael Levi was playing soccer in the street, kick-the-can fashion, with local school children as Lillian and her driver turned the corner on two of their three wheels. Nearly colliding with the rag-tag band of ballplayers and half a dozen cheering spectators, the vehicle sputtered and then came to an abrupt halt with half the chassis on the sidewalk and the other half in the street, the combined result of a failed clutch, a barely responsive hand brake and a divine intervention. Lillian was out of the taxi before her driver could extend a hand of assistance.

"Dad," she exclaimed as she ran to embrace her father from behind, finding herself suddenly surrounded by more than a dozen young street urchins and one overgrown adolescent that the children had already come to know as their *Maestro*, but Lillian knew only as her father.

Two: Michael

January 2008

He slowed his car as he threaded it perfectly between the two small stone pillars identifying the entrance to the paved drive. "Birch Lake Day Camp" the sign read as he made a soft right turn into the day camp property. Michael was told at the Orientation Meeting in early June to park "up on top", but today he wanted to get the full effect of how the campers feel arriving through the entrance on their first day. He wanted to capture the stomach twisting of the fifth grade camper, the uncertainty of a new experience, the feelings that he had experienced forty-two years earlier, when, as a camper at this day camp, he rode through the pillars for the first time. Disappointed, Michael had felt none of those emotions today. He was now looking for something else: the ghost of a ten-year old boy and a ten-year old girl, sitting on the curb near the boys' changing house, exchanging secret gifts and giggly promises. He wrote on a diner placemat later that evening:

Shelley, a camper my age, was looking for her first love that summer. I could tell she liked me by the way she handed me a colorful nametag she made during her arts and crafts period: Three toothpicks glued together served as the background, with the

following Alpha-Bits letters glued to the wood: M-I-K-E, the letters
spelled out my name.   For the long winter months following the
summer of my first love, I nagged my mom to buy Alpha-Bits cereal.
I would arrange the name, S-h-e-l-l-e-y, with my spoon in the sugary
milk. My chin cradled by my hand as I stirred, I imagined scenarios
where I would save her from the perils of camp.   I cautiously
separated the sacred letters from the rest until they became
unrecognizably soggy in the sugary, lukewarm milk, treating them
preciously until they dissolved into the milky nothing-ness. I sat vigil
through those winter months with my favorite cereal, staring out the
kitchen window at the whirling snow, wondering what romantic
encounters future camping summers would bring.

"Mikey, take your lunch. Larry is outside. Have a fun day at
camp."

Larry's car was waiting. There were no camp buses in 1962, or
even seat belts in Larry's car. There was only a teenage driver, a
pack of Lucky Strike cigarettes rolled into his left sleeve, and the
WMCA Good Guys cheerfully talking a mile a minute on the radio.
Too many campers were crammed into that uncomfortable, broken-
spring rear seat. Larry must have been paid by the number of
campers he could deliver in one piece each morning. A cocky hand on
the suicide knob, this newly licensed driver was overconfidence
personified as I was whisked off each weekday to day camp.

The brochures that my parents received in the months before that
summer of 1962 painted a picture of a fun-filled adventure in the form

47

of softball championships, frog-catching, riflery, and more. What the brochures did not paint was that a childhood love affair expressed in sweet cereal letters pasted to a toothpick backdrop had the power to propel this ten-year old kid's ordinary life into one played out on the pages of Archie Comic Books and Hardy Boys Adventure Stories. A childhood fantasized into countless Lone Ranger, Sky King, and Roy Rogers Saturday Morning Adventure Episodes, where the hero gets the girl in thirty minutes minus commercials, only to give her up in the end for a higher calling: one of the solitary traveler riding into the sunset as the credits rolled in the foreground, followed by a few words from the sponsor of the televisions show: "Kids, remember, ask mom for Alpha-Bits, the cereal kids love best."

"Mister, now as then, you don't have to tell me twice!"

Michael had grown up since 1962, and so did Birch Lake. It was now the winter of 2007-08. New owners were on board with modern ideas and in spite of the snow that covered almost everything and was still falling; it was evident that bright new buildings with fresh paint dotted the camp landscape. Olympic-size swimming pools, now empty would soon be ready for the swimmers of summer. There was no trace of the old photography shack, which would have stood to Michael's left as he slowly made a right hand turn and approached the circular drive that served as an off-season parking area. In place of the mildewed bungalow that once reeked of silver nitrate and God knows what other chemicals, stood a rustic shed-like structure with the words "Pottery and Ceramics" wood-burned over the door. Still standing was another bungalow only a few yards beyond the pottery and ceramics area and up a small incline: "The Birch Lake Nature Center" the rustic, creaky sign read, twisting in the wind on brave chains. It was there that Michael spent a frightful night on a camp sleepover. Huddled under a sleeping bag and soaked in shaving cream, he was just one of the many victims of rival campers' aerosol pranks.

"What happened to the rifle range?" Michael wondered as he approached the freshly shoveled entranceway. This first interview would be conducted in the Main House, just yards away from where Michael had discharged his .22-caliper clip, totally missing the small black and tan target, depositing his bullets safely into the sandy hill or the unexplored woods that lay beyond.

" . . . Twenty two-caliber bird guns . . . the ones you handled back then . . . are no longer allowed at Birch Lake for obvious insurance reasons," Assistant Director Dan Crocker explained, sitting back and looking out the window at snow yet to be shoveled. He wrote something down on a pad. After the interview Michael would take another look behind the Big House to where, forty- five summers earlier, he had lied spread-eagle on the hard ground, pointing his rifle at targets propped up against six bales of hay in an area carved out by a backhoe. A climbing wall now stood where the rifle range had lied in wait for gun-slinging hopefuls, the cabled intricacies of a *zip line* ran deep into the woods. Even with the leaves off the trees, Michael could not see where the other end was anchored. "Day camping has certainly come a long way," he thought as he buttoned up his coat and skirted the piles of snow, back to his car.

A college dropout in the early 1970's, Michael enlisted in the Navy, and following basic training was assigned to Fighter Squadron 31 aboard the Aircraft Carrier U. S. S. Saratoga. Looking back on that time in his life, he counted himself lucky to have been exploring ports of call throughout the Caribbean and Mediterranean Seas while his friends back home had already settled into more sedentary lifestyles. After being discharged in 1978, Michael returned to college.

Drinking coffee in the Student Center, Michael overheard a conversation in the next booth and asked, "Professor, are you talking about the Birch Lake Day Camp in Northern New Jersey?"

"That's the one." There was a silence as the two instructors waited to see if Michael had any more questions before they returned to their conversation.

"Let me ask you, do you think I might be able to get that job you're offering?"

"I don't know, but I'll give you a contact name and phone number . . . nothing to lose by trying . . . anyway, there's nothing like a summer camp, huh . . . better call soon . . . those jobs go fast with the college kids looking to book summer work soon as they can, specially camp jobs . . . they go fast."

"So, you say you were here as a camper in . . . ?"

". . . 1962, Dan," Michael finished the question, not wanting to appear too old for the position, but at the same time searching for a way to connect his life to the job description. He didn't think Dan believed him, anyway.

"Maybe you knew Pete, then?" Turning to the camp handyman, he continued, "Pete, when did you begin work here?" Pete was from Mexico. A short man, who spoke English with a heavy Spanish accent, gave the impression of being underweight even for his slight build. To Michael, Pete looked like a man who was straining to appear sober and doing a poor job of it.

"1980, Dan," Pete replied in a high-pitched voice, grinning at Michael, displaying a grill in desperate need of bodywork.

"Well, I guess you two never crossed paths, then." Dan shuffled a few papers on his desk and his body language told Michael that the interview was about to come to an end.

Shrugging his shoulders and then looking out the office window, Dan added, "I don't have anything for you except kindergarten boys. I don't suppose you'd be interested, and there is another day camp just up the road . . . ."

"That'd be fine. The kindergarten position would be ok. Thanks . . . I'll take it."

Michael wasn't sure if he would be able to get out of his parking space; so much snow had fallen in the time that he was in the main camp building. Pete's assistant was shoveling now, creating piles of snow where there had been none before. Before Michael drove away, he looked again for any sign of the ten-year-old boy and the ten-year-old girl, who, in the summer of 1962, mimicked their teen-age counselors and made a secret promise to each other while the strains of *Sealed with a Kiss* playing on every transistor radio:

" . . . *Yes its going to be a cold, lonely summer, but I'll fill the emptiness, I'll send you all my love, everyday in a letter, and seal it with a kiss.*"

"That was Brian Hyland and you're listening to WMCA Good Guy Scott Muni on 660 am radio . . ."

There would be no ghosts for Michael this time around. He was not called for the position, cementing his decision that it was time to chase his dreams elsewhere.

Elsewhere turned out to be Puerto Rico. It had been three years since he vacationed there, and only for a long weekend. Captivated by the tropical culture and the lush scenery, Michael had applied to the University at Rio Piedras, near San Juan, for a visiting professorship. Three years later he secured an interview, likely because he had just published a book of short stories. He was offered a freshman-writing course for the Fall Semester of 2007.

He stepped off the airliner at San Juan International Airport in late August, a week before the semester was to begin. Renting a condominium from a real estate agency he found on line, Michael slipped into the life style that was his Caribbean teaching life. He wasn't due back in the Unites States until the following September, having been granted a sabbatical from the community college where he had been teaching. Growing complacent with his teaching duties there, he was eager to find out how this new change of scene would affect his creativity. His flight to San Juan was uneventful save for a conversation that Lillian found later in his journal:

". . . and furthermore, he seems to have a wooden leg or whatever, making me even more uncomfortable while he adjusts the thing. I want to be moved to a different seat."

"Certainly, sir, I will see what I can do. Yes, there is an available seat in aisle six. Why don't you go up there and sit? I will be along with beverages in a moment or two."

"Thank you." The complainer between me and the very large man in the window seat got up abruptly, and without excusing himself grabbed his coat and his overhead luggage, and left. The very large man at in the window seat slept, or looked out the window, or watched the in-flight movies. I do not remember exactly when, but some time after the first movie I leaned over and asked him what his story was.

"I am a DJ from East Orange . . . on my way to San Juan for a few days to do a guest spot at a club. Then it's back home to rest before going on to Italy to work for a few weeks." It was about that time *that I noticed the DJ had two artificial legs, attached just below his knees.*

"Would you be more comfortable if you removed those?" I asked. "We could put them on the seat between us."

"Wow that sounds like a good idea. Thank you." What happened next was a tribute to human ingenuity. The DJ swiftly unbuckled his limbs. Within seconds they were safely strapped into the seat between us, and the DJ was soon resting comfortably. Because of his considerable size, the passers-by did not notice that this man's legs ended at the knees. Noticeable, however, were the artificial limbs wearing size fourteen Nike Air Jordans strapped securely in the middle seat. When the stewardess passed by with the beverages, I requested two blankets and one pillow. I tucked in the limbs, and slept for the rest of the flight. The last thing I heard before I fell asleep? It was the complainer of course, shouting from aisle six: "stewardess, where's my drink?"

Throughout the fall and spring semester that he taught in San Juan, Michael seldom traveled far from his condo on the eastern edge of Old San Juan, the historic quarter of the city. He ventured out only for a bicycle ride or a brisk walk the considerable distance to and from his classroom at the University. On rare occasions he would take off a half-day here and there, exploring the rainforest south of San Juan.

Otherwise, his activities were limited to inner city exploration, conversations with the locals and writing.

In late February 2008, Michael planned a brief holiday in Cancun, Mexico during the University's Spring Break, the second week in March. Michael welcomed the opportunity to get away from his normal routine. As he walked through the door of his condo one afternoon early that spring, his cell phone rang:

"Hello, Dad? Dad, its Lillian, your favorite daughter . . ."

"I didn't know I had any other . . . Lillian, how are you? What are you up to?"

"Coming to San Juan, that's what! Jack and Dashell are coming with me. How's late March for you?"

"I'm not sure I'll be here, Lillian. I'm going to Mexico for the break. What dates are we talking about?"

"Some time around the nineteenth."

"That might be ok. I would be back by then, but my plans are not firm yet."

"That's ok . . . we'll take our chances. It's the only time the boys and I could arrange to be together. If we don't catch you there, we'll chase you all the way to Mexico if we have to."

"Tell you what . . . if I'm not here to meet you when you arrive, make your way to a restaurant called *Moorings* . . . just ask anyone where it is . . . I'll leave word for you there. Ask for Denis. So where are you staying?"

"I was thinking of the Hilton.   You only live once."

"Good choice, there.   Talk to you soon . . . I love you."

"Love you too . . . bye."

Michael could have told his daughter not to come to San Juan, but he didn't want to miss an opportunity to see his children.   His departure from New Jersey was hasty, and he didn't give himself the chance to say goodbye. His plans weren't finalized anyway, though the lure of Mexico might be too good to pass up.

Denis Rodriguez was the owner and manager of *Moorings* on Ashford Avenue, a popular nightspot and one of Michael's regular evenings haunts. Michael knew he could count on Denis to pass along a message.

Located near the harbor and directly in front of The Marriot Hotel, *Moorings* was always alive with street traffic and colorful characters, it drew tourists and locals from all over the island. He met Denis one evening shortly after his arrival in San Juan when he ventured out in search of a good steak.   A colleague at the University had recommended Moorings:

"Professor Levi?"

"Yes?"

"I'm Denis Rodriguez, the owner here. I read your book and I recognized your face from the picture on the jacket. You and I have a mutual friend in Max Vazquez."

"Oh, yes, Max. Thank you. How are the steaks here?"

"My chef makes a great rib eye. How would you like that?"

"Medium well. What've you got on tap?"

"Let me choose that for you. I'll put your order in and have your beer sent right over." Denis motioned to someone beyond Michael's view. A green salad arrived.

That was all it took for Denis to share life with Michael. "I grew up on a farm in Cuba . . . arrived in Puerto Rico after attending high school . . . applied for a hotel position here in San Juan . . . working as an assistant manager for Best Western . . . saved enough for a down payment to finance this building . . ." sweeping his left arm from right to left, indicating that, ". . . the restaurant, the bar . . . I got all of it in the bargain." Denis again waved his hand in that curious sweeping gesture; a gesture that made Michael feel included in the life story of a man who an hour before was a stranger.

Michael's Havana journal:

On weekends, Moorings fills up with young people as well as tourists from the hotels and the cruise ships. Located in the historic part of the city referred to on tourist maps as "Old San Juan", partygoers gather in front of the main entrance early in the evening. Music spills into the street as the light of day fades behind the mountains to the west. Those who wait inside for a table are treated to a selection of island drinks in the side pub. Frustrated help scurry about try to please everyone with a brief minimum waiting time and just the right amount of bar snacks so as not to spoil appetites. There is a crowded dance floor here, hard-wired with a computerized lighting system that varies the mood to match the music. Travelers who find their way to Moorings add their own flavor to the excitement of the eastern Caribbean nightlife. This hip scene fosters a safe environment without sacrificing the tantalizing party atmosphere, thus attracting partygoers of all ages.

Denis and Michael shared stories over drinks at least once a week during Michael's autumn and winter in San Juan. They spoke little of their past, preferring to focus on more pressing topics such as woman, music and Puerto Rican culture.

"In case I'm not in San Juan when my children arrive, they can fly to Cancun for our reunion." Michael handed Denis a small package labeled, 'for Lillian' ". . . or they can wait for me here until I come back. If the hotel becomes too expensive for my kids, they can wait for me at the condo. The plants would enjoy the company."

"That sounds like a good plan, Michael."

The package that Denis held for Lillian contained his apartment key, a writing journal, and a collection of journal entries on various scraps of paper written in Michael's hand.

Glancing down at what he was holding, Denis said, "I'd be happy to give these items to your daughter, Michael. I look forward to meeting her." Then, "Michael, as a teenager I escaped from Cuba by boat with my aunts and uncles. My brother was not as lucky. He was caught and returned to Havana. He was sent to prison for a year. Michael, you can do me a favor too." On the back of a *Moorings* business card Denis wrote a telephone number. "My sister Gleynis lives somewhere on the outskirts of Havana. At least, she did the last time I heard from her. There is a son, Andre'. He would be of school age by now. Gleynis works at a school there. She's a cook. While you're in Cuba, you might want to check out the part of the city called Old Havana, *Habana Vieja*. It's rich in history, features delicious food and the women, I recall, are beautiful. There isn't a one without a flower in her hair!"

"Denis, what are you talking about?"

"My sister would be a valuable contact for you; that is, if you should ever find yourself in Havana, mi amigo." Denis raised his eyebrows with the suggestion and then fell quiet, taking a sip of beer.

"Well, I don't foresee visiting Havana or any other city in Cuba in the near future, Denis," Michael replied, but he placed the business card in his wallet for safekeeping.

Denis wished Michael good luck on his journey, shaking his hand warmly as he had done whenever the two parted company.

Denis had fallen silent, so he added, "Thank you for the contact, though," continuing to shake Denis' hand with the add-on gestures that only men of the Caribbean would understand. Without another word, Michael turned to leave the restaurant.

"Oh, Michael, if you do speak with Gleynis, tell her that I am all right, and ask her if there is any word of Enrique'. I would consider it a great favor."

"Enrique'?" Michael asked, turning.

"Yes, as I told you, my brother did not make it out. He's still in Cuba."

"All right, Denis, but I don't expect that I'll . . ."

" . . . And do me one more favor: ask Gleynis to give this to Enrique'."

Denis handed Michael a small gold charm fashioned in the shape of a heart. Michael examined it turning it over in his hand and dropped it into his pocket where it fell among his coins.

Denis continued, "My brother gave that to me before we left for Florida. You might say that it's brought me a bit of luck. If you don't run into Gleynis, pass the charm along to a loved one of your own when the time is right."

"All right, my friend . . . whatever you say. For now I'll keep it right here in my pocket with my change." Michael tapped the right front pocket of his jeans twice. "...I 'm going to need a bit of luck myself if I'm ever going to get out of San Juan."

"You never can tell which way the wind might blow, mi amigo," Denis said softly as he watched Michael exit through the doorway. "You never know," he whispered again, his voice trailing off. Michael was long out of earshot, his mind moving on to Cancun and the notion of a few days of rest and relaxation.

Michael watered his plants and opened the kitchen window a crack. Grabbing his small travel bag waiting for him in the hallway, he turned and locked the door placing the key above the door jam. The cab driver was beeping his horn at the end of the walk. The fragrances and lush colors of gentle hibiscus, oleander and bougainvillea escorted Michael to the curb. He felt a wave of positive vibrations sweep over him as he climbed into the back seat.

Michael was traveling with Max Vazquez, a fellow professor at the University of San Juan. He taught bilingual studies in the Education Department. The traveling companions would meet at the terminal gate. Max was born in Cuba. His family moved to the United States in 1968. He could not remember the exact date when his family traded their homeland for a new one, but he knew it was just before his birthday. As Max grew up his father told him, "In Cuba in those years, you got out if and when the getting was good, *hijo*."

Educated in the United States, first in Miami and then in New Jersey, Max settled in Puerto Rico with his wife, Joyce, and their daughter, Isabelly. He and Joyce found the Eastern Caribbean climate and the employment opportunities in Puerto Rico perfect for starting their family. The young couple had no trouble finding teaching positions in the primary schools and later at the college level. When Max and his wife separated, Joyce returned to New Jersey with their daughter. At first, visitations were infrequent. Eventually however, Isabelly spent more and more time with her father, and as she grew, she made plans to attend the University in San Juan when she finished high school.

Michael and Max were sharing a room at the *Cancun Hyatt Caribe'*. They would be in Mexico for six days, returning to San Juan in time to prepare their lessons for the summer classes at the University. Michael was involved in negotiations to purchase a foreclosed condo in his complex that his real estate agent had acquired at auction. The agent was eager to close the deal before the heat of the summer. Another few weeks and the market would fall flat. If Michael did not purchase the property, it was doubtful that anyone else would show an interest until October. Michael had no plans to extend his stay in San Juan, but even if he returned to New Jersey, he could still purchase it now and lease in the future.

"The condo would make for a good investment," the agent told Michael.

"The condo would make for a good investment," Michael repeated the agent's words to Max one evening as they planned their trip.

Michael and Max sat down to dinner at "O", the main restaurant at the Hyatt, on their first night in Cancun:

"You know, Michael, Cuba is less than an hour from here by air. We could put our plans on hold, fly to Havana for the weekend and be back here by Monday. What do you say? Pass the steak sauce please." Max was not looking up from his plate.

"Oh, sure, that's a great idea, Max. That way, we can spend the rest of our vacation in a Cuban jail. Salt, please."

"No, that's not the case at all. Americans are welcome in Cuba, but Americans do not want to go to there. See what I mean?"

"No, I don't see what you mean. Pass me the salsa, *por favor*."

"I'll tell you what: You think about it, and I'll cover the airline. You just pick up the visas."

"Pass the pepper," Michael said, ignoring his friend's suggestions. "Are you going to eat that?" Michael pointed to Max's untouched salad.

Max passed Michael the salad bowl. "So what do you say?"

"I could use some more water."

"So?"

"If we are going to Cuba, we would need to get some rest," Michael shot back after he finished chewing. He finished the last of his glass. "On the other hand, what the heck, let's have another drink."

" . . . Sounds like a good idea," Max downed the last of his beer.

Michael raised his hand to signal the waiter.

"Wait, Max, I need to leave something with the concierge. You get the taxi. I'll be along in a minute."

"Miss, please give this note to my daughter, Lillian Levi, if she checks in."

"I'll take care of that for you. Thank you for choosing Hyatt."

"Thanks . . . You're welcome . . . appreciate it."

"Will you be returning to us within the week? I can arrange to hold the same room.

"I think so. Yes, thanks."

Michael felt nervous as he approached the Immigration and Customs Area at Jose' Marti International Airport. "If Max is concerned, he doesn't show it," he thought as he watched his friend converse in Spanish with the customs agent. Except for an anxious moment when their visas and passports were closely scrutinized for authenticity, the two Americans passed muster, and as they were shown through the sliding doors of the airport exit. Michael let out a deep breath as his anxiety melted away. Bursting into the afternoon sunlight, they were immediately set upon by a hoard of taxi drivers, each eager to earn a fare by taking on the obviously American travelers as their next fare. "Max, you know Denis Rodriguez, the owner of *Moorings* down at the beach? He suggested we find a hotel in Old Havana. What do you think?"

"That's as good a place as any. Let's check it out."

"*Senor, usted puede tener para nosotros en el Hotel Tejadillo Havan Vieja?*" Max asked the driver. The driver nodded. "So Michael, how did this Denis know we'd be coming Cuba?"

Michael shrugged. "No idea . . . you didn't say something to him?"

"No, why would I say something to him? I don't even know him."

"Well, he seems to know you pretty well."

"Nope, may have seen him . . . that's about it."

"Curious." Michael looked out the window as their driver slowed down and made a turn off the Malecon' and on to a side street.

The Hotel Tejadillo was a great choice for any lodger. Michael and Max were pleased from the first. It had a peculiar layout with a range of accommodations and employees that made them feel welcome. The warren-like floor plan was composed of three restored Havana mansions dating from the 18th and 19th centuries. The location suited their needs. It was situated one short block from Cathedral Square, *Plaza de la Catedral*, and the corner street-level bar had tall windows facing onto San Ignacio and Tejadillo Streets, where passersby frequently stop by for a drink. Young children ran in and out of the open doorway to retrieve errant soccer balls that found their way in from the narrow street where they had been playing their pick-up games. The hotel had two courtyards; one with tables for breakfast fare and afternoon drinks prominently displaying a large and slightly overpowering mural of colonial architecture, and the other courtyard full of marvelously bushy ferns and a yagruma tree whose vast leaves occasionally crashed to the ground, startling unsuspecting dinner patrons and bystanders. The entrance hall was lined with a number of tall windows, traditional colonial window grilles and fanlights, high ceilings and chintzy armchairs. The rooms were decorated with paintings by local artists and with bonsai trees, which held a fascination for Old Havana interior designers. The staff proudly pointed out historic points of interest within the hotel to all who would ask and the entire environment was clean and welcoming.

Sunday, March 9

"Let's eat! I'm starved."

"Me too . . ."

It was already mid-afternoon, and they had not eaten since Cancun. At the desk clerk's suggestion, Michael and Max walked one block to the picturesque *Plaza de la Categral*, where they took a table and ordered sandwiches and beer.

Returning to their suite of rooms that evening, there was a knock on the door: it was the Bell Captain. With him were two young women. Michael thanked the bellhop for his courtesy, but refused the offer of their services. He gave the bellhop and the women each ten pesos for their trouble, and sent them away. The Bell Captain shrugged and ushered the girls away. He said he would return later in the evening, to see if the Americans would be interested in company. True to his word, he returned later with the same two women. They were dressed differently on this visit, and smelled good. Michael invited them in, tipping their indifferent escort before closing and locking the door.

Monday, March 10

"Michael, you can't be serious? What are you going to do by yourself in Havana?" The taxicab pulled up to take Max to the airport. Michael and Max had walked outside with their coffee cups, with a nervous busboy following behind.

"Oh, I'm sorry, amigo. Here you go." Michael surrendered his cup, but not before draining it of every last drop. Max did the same. "I don't know . . . a little research for a book, maybe." He fingered something among the coins in his pocket. "I'll only be here a few days. Then I'll catch up to you in San Juan before the start of the new semester. Max, do me a favor: When you get home, would you water my plants and open the windows in my condo a crack? I think I opened them before we left, but I don't remember. The key is above the door on the jam."

Michael had enough money to extend his stay by only a few days. He entered Cuba with a few thousand pesos, and even fewer euros. Any more he would have had to declare at the Customs window and that would have meant paperwork and unwanted exposure. Michael was hoping that Lillian had at least gotten as far as Cancun. If his daughter were reluctant to fly to Havana, perhaps the money in the envelope would help convince her to make the trip.

" . . . Michael, if you do speak with Gleynis, tell her that I am all right, and ask her if there is any word of my brother, Enrique'. I would consider it a great favor . . ."

Michael was thinking of his friend's words the last time he saw him. Taking the *Moorings* business card from his wallet, he dialed the number that was written on the back. The phone rang five times before a woman picked up:

"*Ola*?"

"Gleynis Rodriguez?"

"*Si*, this is . . ."

Three: Gleynis

Gleynis Rodriguez was born twenty-four years ago, the youngest of three children, near Santa Clara, Cuba, on the farm where her maternal grandfather had made his stake and raised his family. The area had been a modest yet self-sustaining farming community even after Castro seized power.

An excellent student, she set her sights on medical school at the University of Havana. Entering school as a freshman in the fall of 2002, her future seemed bright by Cuban standards. She eagerly settled into her studies and actively participated in the whirlwind of approved clubs and sorority activities.

At a social gathering, she met Mauro Gutierrez, a dark-skinned, free-spirited sophomore, and they began dating. By the following summer, Gleynis was pregnant with his son. Shortly thereafter, Mauro broke off the relationship, all but disappearing into the fabric of the University Community. Gleynis remained in school as long as was practical. She withdrew from the University to finish the third trimester at home with her family.

Making herself a promise that she would return to school immediately after she was done nursing, one year turned into three, as time passed all too quickly.

Gleynis named her son Andre', after her great grandfather, a French adventurer who came to Cuba in the nineteen thirties, and who, while working as a farm hand, had saved enough money to purchase the forty-five acres of land that her family still called home. Although Castro's henchmen had seized ownership of the property in 1962, the Rodriguez family was permitted to remain, working the land, accepting subsistence wages, surviving on what produce they held back from the farm markets. Gleynis' family was still plowing the fields when she entered college, although the tractors and harvesters had long since been replaced by work horses and other less sophisticated means of harvesting.

Today only abandoned farm machinery tells the tale of a once automated and sustainable farm. Machinery was never replaced with age. What engines and mechanical devices that could be maintained with Soviet parts over time were still working. The rest was strewn about the acreage, a rusting testament to the human, political and economic failures of Castro's Cuba. It is said that the Rodriguez farm machinery can be seen from the sky as airliners land and take off in Havana, the airline navigators charting their course by the strewn-about relics on their approach and departure from Jose' Marti Airport.

At one time the family's produce was well known for its quality, size and value. Their vegetables were always in demand, eagerly bought up in the farmer's markets and the grocery stores not only in Santa Clara, but also at the markets of Havana as well as throughout Cuba. Gleynis spent much of her youthful days with her grandmother, Abuela Nan, and from an early age it was generally expected that she would take over the family business because her brother Enrique', the oldest of the Rodriguez children, had no interest in farming. He fancied himself an adventurer like his great-grandfather. Enrique's brother Denis, three years younger than he, was all for going into business-- just not the family business. Both brothers dreamed dreams far beyond the split-rail fence that separated their family's fields from the dirt road that led to town. Gleynis had other ideas too and began saving her pesos for when she would one day have her own medical practice.

"Perhaps I'll become so well known, my surgeon's hand so steady, that I will be invited by Presidents and Prime Ministers to work in other countries, other parts of the world," she told her girlfriend Marisol the evening of high school graduation as they sat in the dilapidated baseball stadium seats, smoking with their shoes off, their graduation dresses faded and frayed from more than one *normal school* celebration.

"Ha, it'll be nothing more or less than what you produce men that will be after," Marisol replied, indifferently, a cloud of exhaled smoke enveloping them and then floating off to the clouds, trailing behind Gleynis' hope, dream and prayer.

She could hear her cell phone ringing as she was finishing the last of the dishes from the morning's breakfast rush. Drying her hands, Gleynis walked over to her brown leatherette fanny pack.

"*Ola, Si*', this is . . ."

"Yes, my name is Michael Levi. I was wondering if we could meet at your convenience. I have a message for you from your brother, Denis."

"Denis?"

"Yes, I have a message for you from Denis Rodriguez."

"Si. I work here at The *Escuela Jose' Machado Rodriguez* on Calle Tejadillo. Do you think that you can find it?"

"Yes, I think I know where it is," Michael lied.

"Good. You may come tomorrow. I will see you then. Goodbye.

Tuesday, March 11

After a breakfast of fried sausage, plantains, toast and coffee, Michael asked directions to the Jose' Machado Elementary School. The desk clerk took a local map from the pile of handouts on the check-in counter, and with her pen marked the trail between the Hotel Tejadillo and the school. Michael didn't have far to go. Jose' Machado was on Calle Tejadillo a few blocks from the hotel in the direction of the Malecon'.

"Senorita Rodriguez, por favor."

In the breezeway of the school entrance, a woman was seated at an old wooden desk. The woman did not reply. Instead she pushed a sign-in pad and pencil nub in front of the stranger. She pointed in the direction of the hallway leading away from where she was seated. The word, "Principal" was hand-written on a sheet of paper and taped on the first door on the left. Michael thanked her and walked away. He knocked twice.

"Si?"

"Yes, my name is Michael Levi. I'm here to meet with Gleynis Rodriguez."

The door opened. A tall woman, neatly dressed in a green pants suit appeared and extended her hand.

"I'm Principal Fernandez. How can I help you?"

"My name's Mike Levi. I'm on holiday here in Havana, and wanted to meet with Ms. Rodriguez. I'm acquainted with her family." Michael was hoping that he had given enough information, but not too much information.

"Mr. Levi, you have business with Ms. Rodriguez?"

"No, she and I have never met. I have a greeting for her from her brother Denis."

Principal Fernandez tilted her head in silent inquiry, but Michael did not want to get his friend's sister in any trouble. "I'm an American . . . I live in Puerto Rico," he continued. I came to Cuba for a short vacation. Maybe this is a bad time . . ."

"Senora Rodriguez is a cook here. She's busy at the moment preparing a meal for the children. May I show you around our school while you wait for her?"

"Yes, thank you." Michael peered into each room as the two educators slowly walked the hallways. "What is it that you need here at your school, Ms. Fernandez?"

"Pencils, paper, a computer . . . as you can see, we have little, or none, of everything."

A custodian stopped by the kitchen to refill his coffee cup. "There is a man here, asking questions about you and our school."

"*Gracias,* Juan. *Es nada.* I was expecting a visitor." Gleynis dried her hands on a dishtowel and left the kitchen area. She joined Michael and Ms. Fernandez as they sat talking in a sheltered courtyard that served as a gymnasium and general gathering place.

"Here is Ms. Rodriguez now," the Principal said to Michael." Michael rose at once and extended his hand. Gleynis accepted it willingly.

"I'm sorry for keeping you waiting. The children are our first concern here at school." She smiled and nodded to her superior.

"I'll leave you two, then. Mr. Levi, please come back again."

Michael and Gleynis stood facing each other in nervous silence. Each took inventory of the other. A young woman, 5'-4", about one-hundred twenty pounds, with shoulder length dark brown hair tied back and dark brown eyes gazed upward at a tall, slightly overweight man who was old enough to be her father; a man who made poor clothing choices in the morning, a man who had not been acquainted with a barber or razor for at least a few weeks. "So, you've brought me word about my brother?" Gleynis whispered when she was certain that the Principal was out of earshot.

"Yes, he lives in San Juan."

"That much I already know, Mr. Levi, but this isn't the place to talk. Let's meet up elsewhere when I'm not working. Where are you staying?"

"I'm at the Hotel Tejadillo."

Gleynis walked Michael back to the central breezeway. "I'll meet you at 3:30 this afternoon in the lobby of your hotel. Good bye." She turned and walked away without another word.

Michael left his room at 3:25 and headed to the hotel lobby. He didn't have long to wait. Unlike much of the Caribbean where time is a relatively unimportant concern to visitors, in Cuba everything ran like clockwork and so did its citizens.

"Gleynis . . ."

"*Buenas tardes*. I had to wait for my girlfriend to take my son. He goes to school at Machado."

"What grade's he in?"

"He's in pre-school . . ." Gleynis rolled her eyes. "He thinks he's much older. I'll pick him up at Marisol's on my way home."

"Marisol is your girlfriend."

"*Si.*"

"Would you like a drink before we go to dinner?"

"*Si, gracias'* . . . Senor Levi, you're in Havana by yourself?"

"My name is Michael. Thanks . . . " he said, pointing to himself, "I came here with a friend, Max . . . kind of a long story. He went home yesterday. I'll catch up to him in Puerto Rico in a few days."

"And Denis, is he part of the long story?"

"That's where I am confused. When Denis heard that I was going to Mexico, he gave me your telephone number. I didn't expect to come to Cuba, but here I am."

Gleynis gave him a look. "How well do you know my brother?"

"He owns a place where I go . . . Moorings . . . we share drinks, we talk . . . let's walk a little. We can get something to eat."

Gleynis agreed. "Michael, where did you say Max is now?"

"He went home."

"So you just decided that you would stay here?"

"I know its crazy, but I had your phone number . . . I made a promise to your brother. He asked me to tell you he was doing ok, and wanted to know if you had seen your brother Enrique."

"Enrique?"

"Yes . . . something wrong?"

She did not answer his question.

They arrived at a restaurant recommended by the hotel brochure.

"Here's a spot. Have you ever tried it?"

"I know this place. It's ok."

At dinner, Gleynis came right to her point. "Is this ass?" she asked bluntly.

"Excuse me?" Michael placed his glass of wine on the table staring disbelievingly at her. He paid closer attention to Gleynis' mouth as she formed her words, and assumed that her accent was getting in the way of her English.

"Is this about ass? Is that what you want?" she asked again, without blinking.

Michael held out hope that he misheard her, but this time her English was unmistakable. He looked around. A woman at a nearby table was staring at him.

"You know, do you assume that we'll be sleeping together? Is that what you think I am going to do?" she continued.

"Not at all, Gleynis, I understood from what Denis told me that you would be a great source of information for me . . . of Cuba . . . and he was curious about his brother."

Seeing Michael's reaction, Gleynis burst into laughter. She took a sip of wine shaking her head in disbelief from side to side rolling her eyes all the while.

Michael sensed the mood was about to change. He began to relax again and drank his wine. He may have been taken aback by her frontal assault, but disarmed by her special charm. He was drawn to this woman who could put him off one moment and captivate him the next.

Changing the subject, Gleynis suggested, "Since you expressed an interest to Principal Fernandez about our school, Michael, why don't you come by and spend a few hours? There's so much to do there. You could work a few hours this week and maybe a few the next, before you return to Puerto Rico. When did you say you were leaving?" There was a sparkle in her eye that Michael had missed until now. Gleynis was testing him.

"I was planning to leave in a day or two . . . but what would I do there?"

"What's the matter, Michael . . . afraid you will become attached? You can tutor the younger children in English, for one thing. We always need that. You can help the older children with their soccer skills and other sports. We need that too, *Dios mio*."

On their walk back to the hotel, the dinner companions walked closely side by side, but their bodies did not touch.

"Your son . . . you must be very proud of him," Michael offered, breaking a momentary silence. He slowed his gait, not wanting the evening to end.

"Andre's father walked out of my life the moment he learned I was expecting a child." Gleynis had a way of gesturing where she raised her hand when she told him this and made a kind of a "whisking" motion away from her body, indicating that Andre's father had been swept from her life. Hearing her story, Michael hoped that Andre's father was gone forever.

"Life in Cuba is never easy. Life in Cuba for a mother is . . . doubles,"

"You mean, twice as hard?" Michael offered.

"Yes, thank you."

" . . . Like so many broken conch shells?"

"Did you say something, Michael?"

"Did I? No, go on, "I'm sorry . . .""

"Yes you did. You said something about conch shells."

"Is that important?"

"No, it's just that my grandmother collected them. I still have a few of them."

When Michael pressed Gleynis for more information about Andre's father, she brushed his questions aside with her gesture of dismissal, rolling her eyes in a way that was mesmerizing to anyone within ten feet of their conversation. Insisting again and again that there was no relationship with Andre's father, she would add, "So why discuss it?"

And that was that. With Gleynis, there was finality to her words that gave Michael a feeling of security when he was with her. He imagined making love to her, although she has not given him a reason to believe that anything would come of wishful thinking.

Michael's interest in Gleynis increased with each passing hour of their first date. He made no secret of his attraction to her. In return, she ignored his advances and flirtations. His persistence did not seem to annoy her, however. She gave him the time he needed between the pauses in their conversations to gather his feelings and to make himself the proper fool.

Wednesday, March 12

On his way to The Escuela Jose' Machado Rodriguez long before any
school children were out in the streets, Michael stopped first at the
corner store. "Senorita, do you have any candy I can buy for the
children at the school down the street?" The clerk took a small plastic
bag from under the counter; the type that a customer might receive
instead of a paper one in a supermarket in the states. Removing five
pieces of candy from her bag, she placed them slowly one at a time on
the counter, looking at Michael to see if that was what he meant.

"Wait, no, I need that whole bag. How much? *Quanto es que?*" She
wrote an amount on a small pad with a pencil nub, and handed it to
him. He nodded and took pesos out of his pocket, counted the right
amount and left with the bag of candy. Stopping at another store along
the way, he purchased a soccer ball (the only one they had), two plastic
bats and six wiffle balls. That was all he could carry to the school in
one trip. Anyway, that was the store's entire sports inventory.

"*Mira, ola Senor Michael,*" a young voice called out as Michael
entered the school building. Michael turned in the direction of the
voice. He recognized the child as Gleynis' son from a picture she had
shown to him at dinner the night before.

"Well, young man, *Quel es tu nombre'*?"

"Andre Rodriguez, Senor," he said as he came running up, already out of breath, his eyes open wide to the items Michael was carrying.

" . . . Good to meet you, Andre', he said, placing the bats and balls down and offering his hand. By now other children were gathering and chattering. "Did you know that I was coming today?"

"My mother told me."

"And your mother told *me* that you go to school here."

"*Si, Senor Michael*, and I play soccer," he replied, hoping his confession would earn him a soccer ball.

"Let me see if the next time I come to school I can bring you your very own soccer ball, Andre'. We'll play together. You can show me some of your best moves."

"*Gracias* . . . Thank you," Andre's grin was ear to ear. He left quickly to tell others of his good fortune, waving over his shoulder as he ran.

" . . . See you later." Michael waved back. By now a large crowd of children had gathered, but an older boy came outside to ring a bell, indicating the start of the school day.

Principal Fernandez introduced Michael to a fourth grade-reading teacher. She asked him if he would give the teacher a forty-five-minute break following her first period class. Michael was greeting the fourth grade class when he noticed a girl, no more than three years old, sitting next to a female student, at a tiny desk of her own. She was coloring intensely, her tongue extend from the side of her mouth like a child in concentration will do, her teeth clamped down indicating creative intensity, the crayon bit scribbling with abandon.

83

"And who is this?" the American teacher asked. A young parent-aide in the classroom translated.

"That is her sister," a boy eagerly replied from the back row, pointing to the student in question. Two small dogs, a Chihuahua mix and a slightly larger wiry terrier with one eye walked into the classroom. One yawned while the other scratched.

" . . . And I suppose they are the little girl's dogs?"

"No, they just want to hear the lesson, Maestro." The students giggled.

Michael's Havana journal:

Andre' is a bright, energetic boy; four year old. He plays soccer with the older boys in the enclosed courtyard in the center of the school building. Gleynis is pleased that her son has playmates. "It is good for a boy to have older brothers, uncles, anything . . ."

Andre' and the other young ones wait for their school-age friends to finish their morning subjects, and then join them at recess.

Andre' attends preschool while his mother works her shift preparing breakfast and lunch for the school children, but I think that if Gleynis were not there, her son would not be there either.

Gleynis and the other cooks were able to earn an additional one or two pesos each school day preparing specialty meals for the teachers, school employees and volunteer mothers who helped out as classroom aides and unofficial janitors and fix-it people in and around the ancient school compound. The school could not function without parental help. Some who helped were not much older than the eighth graders, while others could have been grandmothers or extended family guardians.

Laborers and deliverymen would find reasons to show up at the school each weekday morning for a hot roll. "Gracias, Gleynis."

"De nada, Senor Pinto." Butter was expensive. The appreciative visitors were more likely to get homemade jam and a cup of strong Cuban coffee.

As to Andre's father's whereabouts, Gleynis told those who asked only that Mauro had gone away looking for work and had not yet returned. She was afraid to share information about her marital status, fearful that if others knew her personal life someone might try to take advantage of her often-desperate situation and could threaten her with the prospect of losing her job.

There were a few educators from Canada and Western European countries teaching at the school; some of whom began their working visit by staying at the Hotel Tejadillo, moving on to the homes of host families within the community when the money ran out. Those who came to give their time and expertise to the children in Havana and elsewhere on the island would stay for extended periods of time to teach, to perform social or church work, and to even provide rudimentary medical and other health care services.

One young woman at the Jose' Machado School was from Italy. She spoke her native Italian, Spanish and English. She taught foreign languages to all grade levels at the school. A young woman from Scotland was teaching a drama workshop. She was having success with even the youngest of students. From what little Michael was able to watch in his spare moments, he guessed that the second graders were practicing a fairy tale. There was a little girl in a paper mache' dragon outfit. Another girl was dressed as a princess. The cafeteria tables were transformed into their stage after the last lunch was cleaned up.

Volunteers often remained in Havana for more than their contracted period with their host agency. The teacher from Italy's visa could not be renewed again and her stay in Cuba at an end. She promised Principal Fernandez that when she returned the following summer, she would teach the children the conjugation of irregular verbs.

"Just come back," Principal Fernandez said, and gave the young woman a hug.

Friday, March 14

Michael asked the janitor if the school had any musical instruments. He returned with a small guitar that had been all but forgotten in a deep sink closet in the maintenance area off the kitchen. The neck was warped from moisture, but the guitar still had six rusty strings. Michael was able to tune five, but the sixth string, the high "E", had a broken key. Michael and the janitor were able to repair it with a small screw and gear combination taken from a can opener that Gleynis provided.

Thanks to Cuban ingenuity and a modicum of American talent, Michael led a seventh grade class in a round of *La Bamba* and *Guantanamera*, the only two songs that he knew in Spanish. Gleynis heard the singing as it traveled the hollow hallways, and sat in on one of the choruses.

"You knew your way around that one, Gleynis."

"Gracias . . . my father is a musician. He plays with his band here in Havana. I'll take you there."

"Ok, how about lunch tomorrow and we'll talk about it."

"That'd be great, Michael. I'll call *Papi* to see what's going on."

"Ask Marisol to join us."

"I'll ask. That would be good. My mother is not working tomorrow . . . she can watch Andre'."

Saturday, March 15

Gleynis arrived for lunch with Marisol. She distrusted Michael from the start, and made no effort to hide her dislike for him. Displaying little emotion, Marisol carried with her everywhere a cynicism in her approach to life. A chain smoker and drinker, she contributed only minimally to the conversation. Supporting Gleynis with a nod of the head, she sat at Gleynis' side, watching Michael. Gleynis' defender and confidante', Marisol felt responsible for her, and had felt that way since they were children in Santa Clara. Where Gleynis displayed a tough exterior, Marisol was hardened inside. She was the product of poverty, abuse and neglect. Largely abandoned by her family at a young age Marisol was raised by Gleynis' mother and grandmother on the farm. Gleynis' family was there to feed Marisol, get her out of jail when she was sixteen, and to help her with an unwanted pregnancy a year later.

"Ladies, let's get going. Gleynis, should I call a taxi?"

"The bus is just as easy, and it's free."

It may have been free, but the trip was anything but friendly. Marisol rebuffed Michael's attempts at conversation. She looked out the window . . . or smoked . . . or both. Gleynis was cordial, but knew that Marisol was playing her against Michael. Gleynis loved

Marisol . . . understood Marisol, but wished she would be friendly, just this once.

"So, Miguelito, where did you learn to play the guitar?"

"Just picked it up I guess. So your father is an entertainer?"

"Si, la artista." Gleynis threw her head back and the rush of air from the open bus window showed Gleynis' bare neck. Michael noticed she had a small cluster of birthmarks--a constellation of sensual beauty. He had to look away, but the image remained in his mind. He closed his eyes and sighed. When he opened them, the bus had stop with the wheeze of the brakes and a cloud of evening dust. The sign on the little roadhouse said, *Ron*, or "Rum" in English. That was all. Live music could be heard as the threesome stepped off the bus.

The inside of the *casita* looked like the bus stop it truly was. Beyond a few scattered tables and chairs and a cooler stocked with sandwiches, colas and beer, a three-piece band was playing. When they walked in, the musicians stopped.

"Ola, Gleynis!"

"Papi, que tal?" She and Marisol walked over. Michael waited to be summoned. *"Este es mi amigo* Michael Levi. *Yo le dije acerca de usted. él también es un músico de clase* . . .

"So, Senor Levi, you are a musician, eh? Come play with us."

"I'm afraid I don't know much more than La Bamba"

"La Bamba it is . . . uno, dos, uno, dos, tres . . .!"

Sunday, March 16

After an early morning squall Michael walked along glistening cobblestones to a book fair in the local park. The few books that were there were thirty-year old hard covers, and the few vendors present bespoke of an economy that did not value the published arts. The printing was second rate, and most covers were in black and white. The cheaply bound volumes, most with black and white covers, were predominately pro-Communist publications, Ernesto Che' Guevara biographies, and political commentaries on the July 26 Movement or pro-Castro manifestos. Michael engaged in a quiet discussion with a bookseller about Cuba since the Revolution. The two spoke in general terms only, and when police strolled by, Michael drifted to another vendor.

He smiled as he watched a wooden dance floor being laid over the pavement in preparation for the upcoming weeklong music festival. Michael enjoyed the idyllic setting of the park and decided to return with his journal Monday rather than help out at the school. Besides it was his birthday. He would sleep in, have a good breakfast, and catch up on his emails to Puerto Rico.

Michael tried to reach Gleynis by phone to tell her his plans. "Maybe she would like to join me?" There was no answer. Her phone was turned off or she was out of range. He was back in his hotel room by early evening, and after a hot shower, went right to bed.

Monday, March 17

"Max, I expect to return to San Juan within the week. Please inform the University that I am still interested in teaching the summer course. See you in a few days. Are my plants ok? Thank you, Michael."

Gleynis asked Principal Fernandez at the end of the school day if she had heard from Michael. *"Yo no lo he visto,"* she replied indifferently. Raising an eyebrow, her eyes followed her favorite cook out of the office and down the hall.

"Buenas tardes, Senorita Rodriguez," Principal Fernandez called after her.

"Good afternoon, Principal Fernandez," she replied over her shoulder, extending her hand the way she did without turning around. She was already in the street and on her way to the Hotel Tejadillo.

"Is Senor Levi available?"

"Si, Senorita, would you like me to ring his room?"

"May I just go up?"

"Si."

Pointing across the lobby, she continued, "Make a left there and go through the center court. Then up the stairs, turn right, and you'll find his door on the left: Room 214."

"Thank you." Pushing off from the desk like an Olympic swimmer in a tightly contested heat, Gleynis turned and left. She paused to brush out the wrinkles from her blouse and jeans and she shook a mop of curls out of her eyes. She knocked twice, an echoing silence between each one.

"It's open."

Michael was facing away from her as she entered. "Pardon the appearance of the room, I was writing and didn't have a chance to . . . Gleynis? *Ola*. I thought you were the maid service."

"Michael, where were you today? We missed you."

"Yes, sorry, working . . ."

Gleynis noticed the balcony doors first. There were three sets of tall shutter-like partitions, strong and secure in appearance, each standing open to tiny balconies adorned with lush tropical plants in large terra-cotta urns. Removed her bright calico shawl, Gleynis draped her colorful calico shawl over the over-stuffed chair in front of the T.V. There was the sense of being too close to the neighbors across the narrow street even before one stepped out on the balcony.

"These are the images that visitors take with them when they leave Havana," motioning across the Calle', "and the scenes artists paint of the Cuban people. It's how we are pictured by visitors from all over the world. These images inspire writers and poets as they turn out works full of intrigue and romance, of trysts and of pleasant encounters . . . yet all the painting, writing, and good intentions in the world could not begin to tell our stories."

"Maybe our governments are close to normalizing their relationship, allowing for . . ." Michael put in, sounding like a CNN news analyst.

"We're talking about two different things, Michael," Gleynis did not take her gaze away from the Cathedral, the worn and broken saints-in-relief staring back from their massive fortress wall alcoves, their acid-rain tears reaching the unsuspecting passers-by on the narrow cobble stone street below.

Michael was not looking at the statues. He was studying Gleynis' movements as she glided on tiny feet through the rooms of his suite. She was a petite 5'4", and the more he observed her, the more he understood why this young woman needed to be both assertive and reserved. It would take more time to understand why she carried within her such a heaviness of heart.

"Gleynis . . ."

Not waiting for him to finish his sentence and turning to him with her hands on her hips, she asked, "Michael, where were you today? The children were disappointed."

"So that's why you're here. Yes, I missed not being there too. I tried reaching you yesterday. Today's my birthday . . . Gleynis, it's entirely possible that my daughter will arrive within the week."

"Feliz Cumpleanos, Miguel!" She now moved to the kitchenette with its four counter burners, its sink, and its under-the-counter refrigerator. Her mood brightened as she made an overture to her host:

"Oh . . . I can cook for you!" Gleynis made a motion with her right hand as if moving a frying pan back and forth over an open flame. "Shssssh, Shssssh," She made the sound of food sizzling in a pan. Throwing Michael a sideways glance and a smile that came from so far away that he wondered to who it was intended, he was relieved that the current emotional storm had passed. Standing there in profile, mouth slightly open and with lips parted, Gleynis revealed her small, perfect teeth. Her eyes were intense as she spoke, twinkling all the while.

"Your daughter's coming to Havana?"

"Yes, we were supposed to meet in Puerto Rico, but this trip came up."

"Michael, everyone loves to come to Cuba. You'd think it was the best place in the world."

"Well, it seems that way to me, and I know I should have gone to the school today. I'm sorry. I remembered that I needed to send an email to your brother. I wanted to let Denis know that I made contact with you, and that you were safe." Michael glanced sideways at Gleynis for a reaction, as if he were a child trying to put one over on a parent. Gleynis was not listening to him. She continued to move about the room, examining a dresser as if she were an art dealer determining the quality of the piece by the texture of the grain. Pausing, her eyes opened wide. There on the dresser top with Michael's change was a small charm in the shape of a heart.

"Michael, where did you get this?" she walked over and picked it up.

"Your brother gave it to me. Is it important?"

Gleynis placed the charm back down among the change. She did not answer his question. Michael wanted to ask her if she had any contact with Enrique', but decided that now was not the time. Clearing his throat, he managed, "Let's go for a walk and get some fresh air . . . maybe something to eat." Gleynis nodded as she allowed Michael to place her shawl across her shoulders. Exiting together, they moved together to secure the last of the balcony doors. Their hands touched. Sensing the awkwardness of the moment, each backed away, allowing the doors to remain open for a moment. It was Michael who composed himself first and closed them, checking the latch twice to make sure it was locked. Allowing the moment to pass, the awkwardness remained heavy in the air after they had gone; an awkwardness that slipped out silently with the arrival of the maid a few minutes later.

Michael placed his arm around Gleynis' shoulder and escorted her down the winding staircase, but by the third step she was ahead, stopping to wait for him when she had reached the bottom. Strolling casually as if they were old friends, Gleynis shared a story. Michael, hands in pockets the way French men carry themselves in that bohemian way as they discuss poems and politics, leaned into her conversation, savoring every tidbit of information. The couple nodded to anyone in their path, lovers and friends returning from the direction of the Piazza. As they passed beneath the statues in the walls of the Cathedral, there would be no crying saints on such a beautiful evening as this. In these moments all the poverty and sadness on this glorious island that was Cuba evaporated into the Havana night sky, the dark tear-like drippings on the cathedral walls still clearly visible from a distance for those who cared to see.

Saturday, March 22

There was a knock just after 2:30 am. Michael had been out late in the Piazza, returning to the hotel only an hour before. Finishing up his writing, he turned on CNN as he dozed off. Wakened with a start, he heard a faint commotion outside his door.

Gleynis was alternately standing upright and leaning on the door framework. She had been drinking. Her clothing smelled of cigarettes and liquor. Michael helped her into the room, and placed her in a sitting position on the sofa in the anti-room. Turning to the kitchen, he returned with a glass of ice water and two aspirin.

"I feel like . . ." she managed in broken English, but Michael could not quite make out what she had said. He thought he heard the word, "goo". Stroking her head for a moment, he returned to the kitchen to start a pot of coffee. Helping her off with her coat, Michael opened the balcony doors closest to Gleynis, placing her smoky jacket on the railing. The fresh air and comforting sound of percolating coffee awakened her with a welcoming morning aroma. Sitting in silence, she accepted the coffee and forced a grin toward her host.

"Maybe you'd feel better if you took a shower?" Michael asked, studying her.

Sending him a wounded glance, she turned her gaze downward. " *Si, gracias,*" her head now cradled in her hand. "I forgot to give you a bir..." A sip of coffee later, Gleynis tried once more, "a birthday present." She stood and made her way to the bathroom. Michael ran the water as she let her clothes slip onto the bathroom floor. He carefully folded each one, placing them in a small plastic laundry bag. Taking a white terry cloth bathrobe out of the bedroom armoire, he set it on the toilet seat cover. Thinking again, he picked it up quickly and hung it on the hook on the back of the door. Gazing through the translucent shower curtain, Michael decided that Gleynis would be ok by herself. He left the bathroom door open half way just in case she needed to call for help.

Gleynis slept until 6:00 am. She cinched up the shorts Michael had given her for pajamas and knotted his t-shirt across her stomach. Tip-toeing out of the room she walked four blocks to the open-air *mercado* for groceries and fruit. Back in fifteen minutes she went to work preparing breakfast for two. It was now her turn to make the coffee.

Michael was still asleep in the big chair with the television on, the endless ticker tape scrolling along the bottom of the screen. Locating a knife and medium size frying pan, Gleynis diced white onions and a few shitake mushrooms. To this she added two cloves of garlic. Finally, she seasoned with *Adobo*, the favorite forgiving seasoning of many a cook in the Caribbean. After washing and drying an additional sauce pan she saw hanging on the wall more for display than for use, Gleynis sliced four small red potatoes very thin and heated them adjacent to the sizzling morning mix. If there had been more time or another pan, she would have parboiled the potatoes. Salt and pepper

100

were added next as the dish began to imitate the frying sounds Gleynis' had made the day before. The aroma from the kitchen could not be ignored. Michael stirred and walked into the bathroom. He quickly returned to his chair, stretched and closed his eyes, a content expression on his face.

When Gleynis was satisfied that the fixings were just right, she moved them to the side of the pan and began frying four eggs, one for her and three for Michael. Not finding a toaster, she browned two pieces of bread she sliced from a fresh loaf, in the tiny grill section below the stovetop. Checking the cabinet, she found two plates and two sets of utensils, washing them with detergent she had purchased. When the plates had received the food and she was satisfied with the presentation, a bit of sliced orange was added for garnish.

"Good morning." Gleynis gently pushed Michael's leg with her foot, his platter of *huevos, papas*, and *tostas* in one hand-- a cup of coffee in the other.

Opening his eyes, he nodded, stretching and squinting, as if for the first time that morning.

"Oh, come on, Michael, you think I don't know you woke up some time ago?"

Michael smiled as a bright sun now squeezed itself through the balcony doors like morning oranges through a juice maker.

"The Maker of this day could not have taken any more care than the maker of this beautiful breakfast."

"What?"

"Here, take this extra egg . . . everything fifty-fifty. Gleynis, what are you doing tonight?"

"Why do I have the feeling that you are going to tell me?"

"Well, why don't you come back?"

"We'll see. Right now I have to get to *mi hermana's* and pick up my son."

"Hermana?"

"Marisol . . . she might as well be my sister."

Gleynis said goodbye, leaving Michael to the dishes and his imagination.

After picking up Andre', Gleynis visited her mother. "Mami, there is an American at the Tejadillo."

"Tell me something I don't know, little one."

"This American is from San Juan. He says he knows Denis, and . . . the American has a charm. I think it is *the* Charm . . . says Denis gave it to him."

Standing on his balcony enjoying a glass of wine on the Saturday evening before Easter, Michael watched the evening processional make its way past the Cathedral along Calle' Tejadillo toward the main entrance on the Piazza. The Easter Vigil was in full swing and there would be a lighting of the Baptismal Fire.

Gleynis pulled away from Michael's attempt at an embrace and moved back into the room to refill her glass.

"Save your energy, my love. I will let you in on a little secret: when a woman wants to sleep with a man, she'll let him know. This is a simple fact that most men aren't aware of or won't believe."

"Now where did that come from?" Michael drained the remaining of his wine in one swallow and followed her into the bedroom, leaving the doors open. With a familiar wave of her hand, Gleynis indicated that the conversation was, for the moment, over. After refilling his glass, Michael turned toward the balcony doors. Gleynis grabbed his arm, turning him around and pulling him back to her. She held him, kissed him and guided him to the bed; the spilled wine on the bedspread a worry for another day.

Later, wrapped in each other's arms, Gleynis told Michael part of the story of the Charm of the Heart:

"My grandmother, Abuela Gutierrez, gave a heart-shaped charm to her oldest grandson, just before he spirited away in the night sailing secretly from Cuba, to Miami. Enrique being adventurous did not believe in charms so he gave this "Charm of the Heart" to his younger brother Denis. I know this because Enrique' told me when he got out of prison. My family assumed the Charm was lost forever and now here you are, an American in Havana, with the Charm."

"You make my heart beat," Michael said.

"Michael, didn't you hear anything I said? And you have cold feet," Gleynis said, pushing him away with her legs.

"Yes, that's always been my problem."

Kissing him she headed toward the bathroom. Gleynis did not close the door, so Michael looked away. On her way back, she picked up the Charm from the dresser. Lying naked next to Michael, she held the heart-shaped object above her head.

"This is it you know . . . it's my Abuela Nan's, all right."

"How can you be sure? Maybe Denis had another one made."

"No, this is it. I know it . . . this it is the charm that my grandmother gave to Enrique'.

Michael's Havana journal:

She commands those around her in ways that transcend her situation. Every aspect Gleynis orchestrates as if her life were one grand cooking school and she was the Master Chef. Life for her is the eternal movement of the frying pan across the fire: always controlled, always deliberate. Navigating around her conversation I am like a pirate encircling an Armada, pillaging her words, plundering her touch. When Gleynis is not around I talk to her in my head. She makes no demands on me . . . I wish she would.

Michael was remembering his first visit to the Escuala Jose' Machado:

"What do the teachers and students need, Principal Fernandez?"

"We all need pencils, for one thing. We have almost none. A computer . . . as you can see, we have only one . . . it's ten years old and broken most of the time. One of our parents works on computers at the National Museum. He usually can get this thing running, but for how long?"

"Yes," Michael wondered now, "but for how long?"

Each weekday morning Michael walked the streets of Old Havana before reporting to the school. After work he walked what seemed like the length of the *Malecon*, surrendering to the pounding surf that called to him from beyond the safety of the ancient bulkhead. He always returned to his familiar vantage point along the Piazza. Waiting patiently with the pigeons for his favorite table to be free he took his place. Michael would adjust his umbrella and allow just enough afternoon sunlight to warm his face without burning his cheekbones.

Michael told stories to the locals, wrote down many more and worked on notes for a future book; a book about the citizens of twenty-first century Havana; a book of characters and events left languishing and ignored by the rest of the world.

"I have sources we could tap, Senora Fernandez," Michael said, a cup of coffee in his hand. "We have so little here, Senor Levi. Anything would help. Enjoy your *café*."

Michael's Havana journal:

There are few living sources of information from before the revolution, a time when American involvement in Cuba meant gangsters, gambling casinos, and other imperialistic symbols of decadent interference. First- person accounts were not easy to come by. There is so much happening right here, right now in Cuba, but precious little news gets out to the rest of the world.

Someone taped a poster on the hotel activity board:

<u>Manuel Yepe' Will Speak Here</u>

Prominent figure in contemporary journalism, economics and

surviving member of the July 26th Movement

Tejadillo Conference Room

Sunday, March 23, Easter Morning

The weather had turned cooler. There was a fog settling over Old Havana, misting from the river and clinging to the cobblestones. Gleynis was dressed warmer than usual. Andre' wore his only white shirt and clip-on tie. The pavement clung to the coolness of the night before, leaving footprint outlines. An airliner passed low overhead. Gleynis looked up. "There are so many broken hearts to gather."

"Mami?"

"Nada, Andre'."

Mother and son joined Michael for brunch at the Hotel Tejadillo. He was already in the restaurant when they arrived, coffee in hand, making notes.

"Good morning, Michael."

"Morning...Hey, Andre'"

"Marisol said hello."

"No she didn't."

"You're right. She didn't."

The adults drank coffee and shared pastry. Andre' had cereal and chocolate milk.

"Gleynis, I got an email from Denis. He wanted me to ask you if you had any word from Enrique'?"

"Not lately, no . . . Andre', finish your breakfast little papi . . ." She stood suddenly as if to leave but sat down just as quickly. "Enrique left Cuba with Denis and our aunts and uncles on an old fishing boat with two rafts in tow. In those days if you could get out, that is exactly what you did. The plan was to land in Southern Florida where friends and relatives were waiting. I was just a young girl then . . . too young to go," mami told me. "She stayed behind, too. Mami had to care for me, and continue to help with the family business. "One day you will go too, *hija,* she promised. "Enrique's raft was picked up at the twenty-six mile marker and returned to Havana by the Cuban Navy. He spent a year in prison. He was a lucky one, I suppose. Others not so lucky . . . drowned . . . sharks. Some were shot on the spot. We will never know what became of the others. My family didn't hear any of this until many months later . . . sooner or later, you hear things." Gleynis paused . . . sipped her coffee. "Ooh, hot!" She placed the cup down and mixed in a bit of sugar. "When he got out of prison, Enrique' couldn't find steady work. He was offered only the lowest of jobs, even by Cuban standards. Because of his crime he was not permitted to hold a position that paid even the occasional tip. Tipping, although forbidden here, has been what has kept us Cubans going you know, during the time of Castro. Enrique' finally found a job pushing a wheelbarrow of meats, fruits and vegetables from a supplier in central Havana to a restaurant not far from here, more than a mile each way. The last time I saw him he was pushing that wheelbarrow and that was many months ago."

Gleynis took a bite of her roll. She nodded as she said this, not to Michael, but to some unspoken agreement, crumbs jumping off her lips like lemmings to the table-ravine below. "Andre', drink your milk . . . Beber *su leche, hijo.*" She reached over and dabbed his chin with a napkin.

"As a Cuban who had served a prison sentence for treason," she went on, "Enrique' was required to report to the police precinct each working day; an appointment at which he was often detained for over an hour, causing him to arrive late for work. His papers were stamped with the word, *"traidor,"* because he tried to leave Cuba, Enrique will never be allowed to apply for an exit visa."

"What do you think happened to Enrique, Gleynis?"

"Who knows what happens to people like my brother," she replied, shrugging her shoulders and taking a sip. "There are many like him here. They come-- they go. They disappear for a time. Sometimes they return, and sometimes they don't. I'm happy to hear that Denis is doing so well."

"Yes, he found his way to Miami, where he worked in the restaurant business. He moved to San Juan, saved his money, bought a restaurant. Gleynis . . . the heart charm you asked about back at the room . . . Denis told me that Enrique' did not believe in charms, so he gave it to Denis, for luck. Denis told me to give the charm to a loved one. Are you the one he meant?"

"I doubt it. Denis barely knows me. Did you say that you'd be seeing your daughter soon? Give it to her, as you say, for luck."

110

Michael reached out across the tundra into the frozen silence to comfort his breakfast companion. She pushed his arm away. Blinking back the tears, she turned away from him. "Andre', why don't we visit the bathroom before we leave? *Necesita ir al baño antes de irnos, Papi poco?*" She excused herself and led Andre' by the hand away from the table. Michael had a few minutes to think about all Gleynis had said. It was not so much her story that amazed him, but the manner in which she bore the circumstances of her life. When she returned to the table, Gleynis was once again composed. "Now, Michael, can we please just have a *conversation*? One without . . ."

"I'm sorry. I know I ask a lot of questions, and your brother Denis . . ."

"My brother Denis," Gleynis interrupted, "can come and visit one day and ask his own questions if he is interested. We tell our stories to outsiders, but they are only stories. I suggest you take them with you and go back to Puerto Rico."

"Are you saying that we should not see each other any more?"

"*Cual fuera el beneficio de prolongar lo inevitable?* What would be the benefit of prolonging the inevitable? You are leaving shortly, aren't you?" her hand motion already launched as if she were a discus player and the plate of pastry on the table were her disc. Catching herself, she put her hand in her lap and looked quickly away. "It's all right, Michael, I'm just upset."

"Well, it is not all right with me," Michael protested weakly. His hope of showing her even in some small way all she meant to him was shattering like a glass in the sink.

"*Las cosas jamas serian como lo fuereon en Marzo* . Things will never again be between us like they are at this moment," she shot back, regaining her composure, forming her words deliberately, indifferently. She looked into Michael's eyes for a moment, then shrugged her shoulders and looked around for her purse. Grabbing it, she reached for a smoke, but held onto it without striking a match. She tapped the cigarette repeatedly on the table. Michael knew that the discussion was, for the moment, over.

"But I never really had the time to show you . . . "

"Mil anos no hubieran sido suficiente, Miguel."

Andre' returned to the table.

"A thousand years would not have been enough. Let it go. I'll see you at school tomorrow. I forgot . . . your daughter is coming."

"I don't know that for sure, but if she does, I'll come to the school to let you know." Gleynis rose, took her son's hand, and left.

Monday, March 24

Michael had originally planned to meet Lillian at the airport, but changed his mind within the last few days. He had a general idea when she would fly in, if at all, but he had no specific information. Instead, he sent a telegram to the Cancun Airport Information Desk letting his daughter know where he was staying. That way she had the best possible chance of finding him. He wasn't as much concerned about his daughter's safety or his own, but in general it was a good idea not to risk unnecessary exposure anywhere in Cuba. Michael waited that morning in his hotel for news. By mid-day he had the feeling that she would have been there by now if she were coming. He stopped briefly in the hotel bar just before 12:00, before walking to the school to report in with Gleynis.

He was finishing a cup of espresso when he heard the laughter of school children as they came running up the street toward the hotel entrance. It was midday, the sixth grade lunch period, and a few other students were on their way home for a break. Lunch at school was optional, but most stayed, while others used the opportunity to play ball in the alleys and streets near Jose' Machado. Michael's young soccer hopefuls knew just where to find him. Stepping into the street, he joined them as they kicked their soccer ball in front of the hotel. Michael played goalie to his students' forward driving attack. This week, he would show them the offensive moves they would need to penetrate his own seasoned defense.

"Senor Levi!" one child called, throwing the ball at Michael. It went over his head, bouncing out of sight. He was so engrossed in the game that he did not notice the coco taxi's abrupt, smoky arrival. He paid no mind as the young woman hastily paid her driver and in an instant came running toward him. Michael did not hear her voice calling out to him nor did he sense that she was closing the gap between them, so wrapped up was he in the important game at hand. Wrapped up, that is, until his daughter's arms were reaching around him from behind, interrupting his skillful block of an otherwise perfect drive toward the goal.

"Lillian, never run onto the field during a crucial playoff game," he scolded her as he turned. Michael could not hold his stern look more than a moment as he broke into a wide grin, sweeping her into his arms for a big hug and kiss. With one arm wrapped tightly around her waist, Michael escorted Lillian out of the heat of the day and into the cooler shade of the bar just off the Hotel Tejadillo's Main Lobby. Tropical ceiling fans moved the air as he nodded toward the bartender, who responded with a beer.

"Senorita?"

"Coke, *gracias*."

"Lil, would you like to wash up or lie down a bit?'

"No thanks, dad, I'm fine. Let me sit here for a bit. Then we can walk and talk a while or do whatever . . ."

The *Plaza de La Catedral* was a colorful gathering place where locals and tourists came together. It was the perfect setting for getting reacquainted. Father and daughter would share a sandwich with another cold beer and coke.

"So, daddy, what's been happening?"

"Lillian, just wait until I tell you . . . I have been helping out at an elementary school and . . . ."

"Dad, what are you doing here?"

"Where do you mean?"

"Here . . . what are you doing anywhere? Puerto Rico . . . Mexico . . . Cuba?" Lillian stood up and paced behind her father.

"I don't know, Lil, just lucky I guess. I needed a change," he said, turning around to the left and then to the right in an unsuccessful attempt to follow her movements. "Will you sit down already? You're making me seasick. I had to break away. I was dying back there."

Circling the table twice, Lillian finally sat down. She stared at him, waiting for a believable explanation.

"So, tell me, how are you?"

"Good. I have a new job and new plans." I am considering graduate school . . . thinking about journalism."

"That's a good plan, but you are a writer or you're not, with or without a degree to show for your time."

"I hadn't thought of it that way."

"What about teaching for you?"

"I don't know," Lillian paused. "That involves kids, right?"

"That comes with the territory." Michael laughed and chugged his beer. "I've been volunteering my time at an elementary school nearby. There are some great people there. There's a woman . . . her name is Gleynis . . . ."

"So that's it . . . maybe I will have a drink," Lillian cut her father off. "What do you suggest?"

"I see the young ladies drinking *mojitos*. It's an island drink with a little rum in it."

"Ok, I'll try that."

A constant parade of magicians, musicians, and other curious characters were now working the afternoon crowd, earning one or two pesos by posing for pictures with the tourists. The drinks arrived. Lillian tasted cautiously and used her swizzle stick to sink a bit of mint to the bottom of her glass. Her mood improved considerably. Her drink took the tension of the day away. Shaking off the effects of travel the sun warmed and relaxed her. By four o'clock the heat of the day was a memory as the sun dropped behind the slate of the restaurant roof, casting the patrons into shadow.

From where they were sitting Michael and Lillian had a clear view of the meringue' band members as they assembled their instruments for the early dinner crowd. Lillian's exhilaration inevitably gave way to exhaustion and she accepted the waitress' offer to bring her a coke and aspirin.

"Dad, I'm tired. I need to lie down and rest for a while. I am definitely feeling the day." She held her head in an exaggerated way, television commercial style.

"Ok, babe, we're out of here. We can catch the music another night. I'll go inside and take care of the check."

Michael left Lillian for a moment to settle up with the house. Her heavy eyelids told Lillian that her day had come to an end. Tired out by food, drink and conversation, she and Michael returned to the hotel. Sitting down on the edge of the king-size bed, Lillian clomped off her shoes. She stretched out across the bead spread without undressing, and was soon sound asleep. It was then that Michael picked up the room telephone and placed a call to a friend who had been waiting to hear from him all afternoon.

Lillian slept until eight-thirty that evening. "Dad . . .?" Her father was not there. She peeked in every room, tiptoeing, as intruders will do. Unpacking her travel bag, she undressed and ran the water, experimenting with the shower handle to bring the water to its steamiest.

Immersed in the misty soothing spray Lillian felt like a young girl again. The oscillating spurts of water from the nozzle soothed her; the effect massaging away sleep and travel fatigue. Immersed in the moment, Lillian was remembering a time when she would shower with her mother; their naked bodies lathered and rinsed, bath toys mingling with soap chunks, steamy warmth reinforcing a child's security and joy. All Lillian knew about her parents' separation was that her mother asked her father to come to the house and pick up his belongings about two years ago. He hadn't been around much in the years preceding that. While her parents' frequent arguments were usually about money matters or Michael's infidelity, Lillian' rule was, "never ask mom or dad the details", and this was certainly not the direction she wished her reunion with her father would take. There would be no sticky questions to spoil this special time.

"There will be time for questions and answers later," Lillian thought, reaching for a towel in the foggy, poorly vented bathroom. There was a knock on the door. "Lil, did you bring the money?" Michael called out, the intrusion obscenely breaking and entering her thoughts.

"Dad, where did you go?"

"I was out walking."

"What? I can't hear you. Yes, I brought the money, but why the James Bond intrigue?

"I can't hear you, honey . . ."

"What? Don't you have a credit card?" Lillian was vigorously drying her hair, expertly alternating between the thick hotel bath towel and the hair dryer she had brought. Conversing with her father through the closed door with the dryer on was near impossible. She opened it one-handed without missing a precious beat of her expert, vigorous drying action. He was already in the middle of a lively conversation with himself, most of which she did not catch.

" . . . so as a rule, Lillian, Americans do not visit, and due to the current diplomatic status between the United States and Cuba, which is to say hostile at best, cash machines, if you can even locate one, will not accept your money. American currency's not permitted here, nor is it permissible to convert dollars to Cuban pesos. There are diplomatic exceptions, but for you or me, obviously not the case."

Entering the main bedroom without regard for the fact that she was neither completely dry nor dressed, her father, quick on the uptake, closed the balcony shutters without pausing in his auditory.

"Well thank you very much, professor, for what I presume was a lecture on Caribbean economics."

"Lillian, put on your clothes before you go traipsing around in here."

"What time is it?"

"Almost nine thirty. Would you like to go out and walk a bit?"

"Yes, that's an idea. Dad . . . Denis Rodriguez told me you that you have not been feeling well. Is it true?"

"True, dear one, but I'm sure it's nothing to worry about. I'll check in with the bones when I get back to San Juan."

"What's the problem?"

"I'm tired, mostly. That's what this trip is about, I guess."

Tuesday, March 25

Michael and Lillian spent the day exploring Old Havana, peeking in the tiny shops; store fronts of no more than a few hundred square feet of selling space; hollow rooms made even more bare by the precious few items offered for sale on the utilitarian metal shelving. There were a few up-scale shops too, but these appeared as if they had been closed for years. Squinting through smoky, dirty windows, there were toppled fixtures, animal droppings and mannequin body parts.

It was the outdoor markets that controlled the tourist action. Ernesto "Che'" Guevara berets and other souvenirs of the Cuban Revolution were displayed on each table. The government may have been overseen by Fidel and Raul Castro, but The Revolution would forever wear the face of a handsome, bold Che', dressed in a beret and army fatigues, his fist raised in defiant salute. There were plaster curios, too. Few bore the trademark, "Made in Cuba". In a country that would have benefited from an economic boost in manufacturing, these items were made in North Korea or China, and other countries that conducted trade with the island nation.

Wearing an invisible price tag were the women of Havana, their unshaven pimps hawking them as if they were Cuban cigars. Women young and not so young lounged lazily and smoked cigarettes in the doorways of the stone buildings outlining the market place, while

120

others aggressively worked the crowds, grazing the thigh of an Italian shopper here, whispering a promise to a French sailor there.

The *Malecon,* or main roadway adjacent to the seawall, was crowded with big, smoky, vintage American automobiles and belching bus traffic. Lovers and friends on foot, walking arm and arm, talked and laughed on the walkway between the thoroughfare and the turbulent waves of the sea. A teenager might whiz by on an old skateboard, one eye on the pedestrian traffic the other on the lookout for an open purse or exposed wallet.

As Michael and Lillian walked that pathway, they were drenched by the occasional powerful breaker, a monster wave breaching the colonial levee and reaching well past where they stood, to the roadway beyond. Weatherworn, decaying hotels lined their route, the rusty structures watching over Michael and Lillian as the two moved briskly under the Caribbean sunshine; a sunshine growing in intensity as each hour passed. These once proud structures, built and maintained with American money and lofty promises, were now without an underpinning of financial stability. This corridor now stood eerily silent; ghost-like sentries abandoned by American and other foreign investors during the nervous first years of The Revolution. These archaic tributes to decades of Caribbean prosperity kept the watch like sailors' wives, staring out from their widows' walks to sea, desperate for a sign of their seafarers' return. By late afternoon father and daughter were worn-out. The exercise and the salt air contributed to the exhilaration each felt.

Michael's Havana journal:

At five thirty on Tuesday evening Lillian and I left the Hotel Tejadillo on foot. Our destination was the Parke Central Hotel; an opulent landmark built in the early nineteen hundreds and continually modernized between nineteen thirty-three and nineteen fifty-nine; the decades that Fulgencia Batista was in control of Cuba. Lillian and I were to meet Gleynis and Marisol for dinner, but I did not know how to bring up the subject.

"Dad, you ok? You seem nervous."

"No, I'm fine. Say, Lillian, listen . . . ."

She was stirring the swizzle stick in her mojito, plotting the most efficient method of extracting the mint leaves and placing them on her tongue for a little extra "zing". With her chin in her left palm and her elbow resting on the table, Lillian poked at her garden salad. She felt about as content and comfortable as she could ever remember. That feeling was not going to last much longer. She saw them out of the corner of her eye as they came through the main lobby doors: two young women, craning their necks, clutch purses in hand. One pulled on the sleeve of the other and the two began walking in Lillian's direction. Michael rose to greet them as they stopped three feet from the table.

"Gleynis, this is my daughter, Lillian."

Lillian looked up and stared. Nodding and placing her salad fork on her plate, she stood up and extended her hand. Gleynis did the same and introduced her companion.

Lillian revealed nothing of her surprise as she greeted the two young women warmly, as if they were old friends. Dressed in almost identical tops and skirts, the two petite, dark haired women looked no more than twenty-one or twenty-two years old.

"It's a pleasure to meet you both. I love your outfits."

Michael shot his daughter a glance, said nothing, and looked around for a waitress. He sat down and put his napkin in his lap, adjusting his silverware.

Marisol leaned in close to Gleynis and whispered something. Gleynis looked at Lillian, nodded, and smiled, burying her face for a moment in Marisol's sleeve. Lillian caught the gesture. Her smile, however, did not leave her face.

"The outfits that you are wearing," Lillian asked again, "where did you purchase them? I would like to take a top like that back with me. Never mind . . . we can talk later."

Lillian rolled her eyes and took a sip of her drink. If she realized she was making a slurping sound, it did not stop her. The waitress appeared.

"Ladies, what will you have to drink?" Michael asked.

"*Lo que las dos senoras que han de beber?*" the waitress helped.

Gleynis and Marisol didn't hear either translation. Appearing agitated they looked around in separate directions. Marisol opened her purse and took out her cigarettes. On that cue, Gleynis searched for matches.

"They'll need a few more minutes, thank you, miss. Excuse my manners, ladies . . . please sit down." He pulled the chairs out for his guests. His eyes were now on Lillian, who by this time was staring back, tinkling her ice too loudly, and nervously tapping a foot.

"Sorry for not saying anything," he mouthed in her direction, and then quickly looked back at the ladies, nodding with a deferring smile. The waitress returned. This time without waiting for an answer, Michael ordered two pina coladas. It did not go unnoticed to Lillian that her father knew what Gleynis and Marisol would be drinking.

"What for you, Lillian? Would you like another?" he asked, looking straight into his daughter's eyes as he spoke to her, holding his gaze there for an excruciating moment.

"Lil?" he asked again.

"Yes, Dad, thank you," replying slowly and deliberately to prolong her father's discomfort, nodding all the while. She then raised her empty glass to him, a ring of melted ice and mint stem on the tablecloth where the glass was once resting.

"And I'll have . . . a beer. Thank you." Michael opened and closed the drink menu quickly, snapping it shut. He had not read it.

The waitress returned with the drinks. She also brought two more small green salads, placing them in front of Gleynis and Marisol. Even the waitress knew the preferences of her father's young dinner guests. Lillian returned to her dinner, looking at her plate and peering up from her lettuce as she slowly chewed, a lock of hair now and then fell into her eyes. She shook it away as she ate in silence.

"So, Dad, how are things going over at the school?" Lillian asked as she singled out and speared a black olive, twirling it as she spoke. Michael did not answer, offering his daughter a look that said, "Leave it alone!"

Turning to Gleynis, Lillian asked, "I understand that you work there as well?"

"*Si, El Escuela Jose Machado Rodriguez*."

"Ladies, if you will excuse me I think that I'll get my name on the email list at the Business Center." Lillian stayed alive in the sea of small talk, doggie paddling until her father returned fifteen minutes later with a lifeboat.

"Well, ladies . . . desert?"

Two musicians came to the table. Michael asked Gleynis to request a song, which she did: "La Bamba", the popular dance number that her father had played for them just days before. The musicians broke into a hot rendition:

"*Para bailar La Bamba, Para bailar La Bamba, Se necessita ua poca de gracia . . .*"

Gleynis and Marisol sang and clapped through two verses. Michael joined in on the third. Soon other patrons joined in. This was enough for Lillian. She grabbed her purse, said, "Excuse me," and walked away from the table toward the exit doors. The music stopped and Michael looked at Gleynis. She nodded and Michael followed her. A sneer crossed Marisol's lips and she whispered something to Gleynis. Michael returned a few minutes later, alone.

"Ladies, we'd better get going. It's been a long day for all of us." He gave Gleynis money for cab fare, and finding the musicians at another table, thanked them for their music and gave them a peso each.

"Gleynis, I'll see you tomorrow. Please enjoy the rest of your meal. Marisol?"

Marisol nodded.

"Goodnight, then," he said again. Gleynis' eyes escorted Lillian's father out of the hotel.

Michael and Lillian walked briskly through the streets of Old Havana and back to their hotel, a distance of less than one kilometer. The cobblestones led through a narrow maze of commercial and residential streets that still baffled his sense of direction. Lillian was not talking, but she seemed to know where she was going: she marched on ahead of her father.

"Lillian, I'm not sure we should have made a left there." Michael tried in vain to break her mood; nothing.

Wednesday, March 26

Lillian hadn't said more that two words to her father since leaving the restaurant the night before. They ate their breakfast in silence.

"Lil, if you're staying much longer, I'll get you a room of your own. How are you sleeping on that other bed?" He was referring to a small day bed in the room close to the entry door, a bright, airy combination of sitting room and kitchenette.

"It would be fine if you didn't snore so loud. You can get me that room tonight! So, you and Gleynis are lovers?"

"No, it's not like that. I told you . . . Gleynis is Denis's sister. He suggested I get in touch with her as a way to learn about Cuba, and she's been my introduction to the ways down here.

"How did he know you'd be coming to Cuba? You said you decided that after you arrived in Mexico. I suppose that introduction included lusting after her? Dad, she can't be more than twenty!"

"She's at least in her early twenties. Why don't we just go to the school together today? The people in charge there are wonderful, and they'll put you right to work."

"I don't want to be *put right to work* for a few days. I came here to see you. We don't have a whole lot of time."

"Time's a tricky treasure, daughter. We can only hope that there is enough of it to make things right in our lives."

"So what's that mumbo-jumbo supposed to mean . . . ?"

"Later." With a wave of his hand, Michael indicated that the topic was no longer open for discussion. Lillian wanted to ask her father if the extra money he requested in his telegram was meant for Gleynis and not for her, but she let the moment pass. She was afraid of what the answer might be, so attached had she become to her father in the last few days, and how jealous she would be if she learned that she was sharing her father's affection with another woman. Besides, Lillian could not resist the chance to visit the elementary school. She was curious what might be holding her father's attention there.

"Will Gleynis be there?"

"Yes, of course."

"Dad, was the money . . . the money from the hotel for Gleynis?"

"I am afraid not, daughter. Cuban citizens are forbidden to have any money at all save what they are issued each month from the Government. The currency you and I carry is for foreigners only."

Lillian and Michael spoke little during the rest of their meal. The delight of juice, coffee, eggs, sausage, fruits and bread did little to defrost the remaining chill in the air. They brushed their teeth and grabbed their journals.

"Are you ready, spaghetti?" Michael asked playfully, grateful that his daughter's mood seemed to brighten a bit after they ate.

"Ready, but you promised me that room tonight," Lillian replied, surrendering a smile to her father and accepting a hug.

"Let's get to *Escuela Jose' Machado Rodriguez*, then. We don't want to miss first period."

The Escuela Jose' Machado Rodriguez was a complex of several consecutive store fronts at street level and similar spaces above, to the height of three stories in some places, and up to five stories in others. The school was not far from Michael's hotel on Calle' Tejadillo, and just a few blocks from the Cathedral Plaza. Overcrowded classrooms serviced a few hundred students in a dilapidated, antiquated setting. The school was in need of absolutely everything. Cosmetically unattractive and unsafe structurally with walls of peeling lead paint and windows without panes of glass, the school illustrated perfectly the poverty that was Cuba.

Classes were already in session when Michael and Lillian arrived. As they approached, the storefront classrooms were visible from the street level to passers-by. If students with windows facing the street were distracted from their lessons, it did not appear to interrupt their concentration. Delighted visitors waved at the children and snapped pictures to accompany the stories that they would take to friends back home.

Tourists asked permission to give the children sweet treats and school supplies that they had brought. With a nod from the teacher, and sometimes without, tourists handed bags of candy, pencils, pens and pads through the non-screened windows to eager hands. Students were permitted to accept the gifts, but all the items would be evenly distributed following the lessons.

For the most part, the teachers good-naturedly allowed the digressions, naturally grateful for the useful items. Therefore the generous offerings were almost never refused, but once the distributions were made, or the materials were stowed away, the students would return to their normal school day, pausing at times for pictures with their teachers before leaving school later in the afternoon.

Moreover, the teachers would politely answer questions visitors shouted through the windows about the building or the curriculum, but if the questions became personal or political, the teacher smiled and closed the windows allowing the students to return to their work without further disruption.

Lillian and Michael found Principal Fernandez in the breezeway as they entered. She was holding a stack of faded copy paper, handing them out to a small group of visitors.

"Principal Fernandez, this is my daughter, Lillian."

"Ms. Levi, welcome. If you're staying, would you mind giving Gleynis a hand in the kitchen? Solimaris is out today and . . . here . . . you might want to read about our school and how it got its name:"

. . . Born in Manzanillo on September nineteenth, nineteen thirty-two, Jose Machado Rodriguez was the son of Jose Machado Hernandez, a lawyer and poet, who worked as a judge in Manzanillo. His mother was Lidia del Carmen Rodriguez Tamay, a fellow campaigner for the Revolution.

"Machadito," as he is affectionately referred to now as then, learned to read in a humble little school district, then went to college. A socially conscious student, he possessed an exquisite poetic temperament with high concepts, and actively engaged in literary activities, along with other young people of similar interests. He took part in the attack on the Presidential Palace on March 13 th, nineteen fifty-seven.

Machadito was a true hero in this action, with the aim of toppling the bloody regime of the dictator Fulgencio Batisa Zaldivar. Injured with a thigh wound from a firearm, he was assassinated along with companions by the henchman Esteban Ventura, April twentieth, nineteen fifty seven.

"Lillian, honey, I'm leaving a little early this afternoon . . . have some things to take care of. Can you find your way back?"

"Sure Dad, no problem. I'll ask directions if I get lost."

"No, I'll send a coco taxi for you."

"Thanks. See you later."

Lillian was helping to prepare lunches when Gleynis asked her if she would meet her for a drink that afternoon after work.

"That's a great idea. Thank you." Lillian was caught off guard by Gleynis' overture.

"Gleynis, I'm sorry that I overreacted last night. I must have been tired."

Gleynis touched Lillian's arm. "We'll talk later."

On the ride back to the hotel after work, Lillian wrote in her journal:

Who is this woman and why is she interested in my dad, if interested is what you call it? She is young and attractive, but who is not good looking or does not carry the aura of mystery on this island? Any way, the woman I worked with today was not the woman I met at dinner.

. . . Lillian stopped writing to fix her hair. Wolf whistles chased the coco taxi the length of Calle' Tejadillo. In no hurry, Lillian tapped her driver on the shoulder, motioning him to slow down. She looked in every window as they drove by, studied every face that blurred the landscape.

. . . And what an attitude she has! She moves right in to speak her mind, yet keeps me at a distance. What was all that business at dinner with her girlfriend not answering my questions? What is her companion to her? We'll see about this.

Gleynis was joined by Marisol at the bus stop which was near the tiny flat where she and Andre' lived. There would be no taxicab ride tonight. That required money, illegal money, and they had not *really* worked, in many days.

"Hola, ¿qué pasa?"

"Hola, no mucho." What did you think of Lillian?"

Shrugging, Marisol did not answer, but lit a cigarette, took a deep drag, exhaled.

"Tu?"

"I'm not ready to say. She seems nothing like her father. I don't want to talk to her about Michael. I know she thinks I'm out for something."

"Aren't you?" Marisol quipped, facing away from Gleynis, taking another drag, and holding the smoke deep before exhaling.

"Absolutely not," Gleynis returned, smiling, shrugging her shoulders, reaching for a drag of her friend's cigarette.

Lillian chose a table some distance from where the meringue' band members were assembling their instruments. The music was a welcome backdrop, but Lillian wanted to concentrate on the anticipated conversation. She took out her journal, intending to record her impressions of the evening, but just then Gleynis and Marisol appeared in the Plaza. Lillian waved to them and stood up as they approached her table. Gleynis greeted Lillian with a smile and a kiss.

Marisol offered her cheek. "I have an appointment in this part of town. Gleynis and I shared the bus ride. I'll return in one hour." Marisol then nodded to Lillian and walked away.

Gleynis waved goodbye. "Don't be too long, Mari." She watched her girlfriend for a long moment as she moved her chair closer to Lillian's. Lighting a cigarette, she took a deep drag, held it in as long as she could, and exhaled. The billowing smoke wafted well beyond the multi-colored umbrella that was anchored in the middle of their table.

"Sorry . . . would you like one?"

"No thank you . . . *Buenes tardes. Que pasa usted*?" each syllable to be judged on its own merit.

"I'm fine, thank you, and that was excellent pronunciation," Gleynis offered in English, also taking time with each syllable, her wide open eyes an invitation of friendship.

"What would you like to drink, Gleynis?"

"I see there that you are a writer like your father," motioning toward Lillian's journal. Mojito, *gracias*."

"Yes. I'm thinking of that, but not like my father," Lillian laughed. "He's the romantic one." She tinkled her glass in the direction of the waitress and mouthed, "mo-*he*-to."

"Lillian, how do you feel about me seeing your father?"

Lillian, spitting a piece of ice into her glass, stared at Gleynis.

"Your father has taken me on a date. Do you object to that?"

"You and my father met a few days ago, right? Do you mean that you're dating?"

"Michael works fast and has expressed interest in me. Here people come into each other's lives and leave just as quickly. That's the way it is."

"Well, I hardly know my father's needs or intentions. I haven't seen him for some time. No, I certainly don't object to his being with you." Lillian didn't know what else to say, so she took another long sip of her

134

drink, rolling her eyes up and into her eyelids. In her head she was happy for her father; in her heart, she felt betrayed.

"I don't pretend to know him better than you, Lillian," Gleynis took out her pack of cigarettes and once again offered one to Lillian. She waved them off. Gleynis worked a cigarette out of the pack. Tapping it twice on the Plexiglas table, she lit it, inhaled deeply, and held the smoke within her lungs like a swimmer going for the record. She gazed beyond Lillian to the steeple of the cathedral across the plaza. Lillian followed Gleynis' gaze. Pigeons were gathering in their celestial roosts.

Lillian and Gleynis both kept their feelings in check as they stepped cautiously through the conversation like soldiers in a field of heart land mines. The two shared drinks and sampled cheese, their swizzles the sticks they used to detonate intellectual traps at every turn. In this manner the hour passed quickly and Marisol returned as she had promised. Taking a seat and raising her hand, she caught the waitress' attention.

"Marisol, join us for a drink," Gleynis offered.

"Don't you see that I am already ordering?" Marisol replied curtly, now in a grumpy mood.

"¿Hay un problema, la novia?" asked Gleynis. Marisol gave her a look, but did not answer.

Lillian picked up on the change in the weather and lightened up the conversation. "Ladies, I'd like you to be our guests this weekend. Would you show my father and me a bit of Havana?"

Pausing in mid-sip, Gleynis looked up and nodded. She grabbed her straw and went back to her sipping. She looked at her companion, nudging for support.

Marisol nodded slowly, "Are you sure it's something your father would want to do?"

"He absolutely would! He's constantly reminding me that I must see more of your city."

"Then we'd be happy to do that," Gleynis filled in Marisol's hesitation.

"Saturday, then, and we can talk at the school in the meantime. We can make plans before the end of the week. I enjoyed our time together tonight."

"That reminds me-- Principal Fernandez asked if you wouldn't mind working the kitchen a few more days. She says you make a good sandwich."

Gleynis and Marisol walked Lillian back to the Hotel Tejadillo, and continued on to the bus stop. Climbing up the sturdy steps of the crowded bus that would take them back home, Marisol leaned into the first seat and said something quietly to two teenage boys who were sitting directly behind the bus driver. The boys looked up and quickly scattered, surrendering their seats.

"I like Lillian," Gleynis said, sitting down next to Marisol, working her butt into the stiff, pad-less seat. Marisol said nothing, offering a cigarette to her friend. The driver depressed the worn clutch and ground the oversized shift stick into gear, causing the noisy, ancient vehicle to pull away from the curb.

It was a damp, spiral bound notebook with a red cover. A notebook that was smaller than the kind a student would use for schoolwork. Gleynis had stored it months ago in a bread drawer; a drawer with broken tracks; a home now for a telephone book, a screwdriver, a few band aids and a dried out tube of first aid cream. There were fuzzy bits of paper attached to the flimsy metal spiral where pages had once lived; high school pages . . . pages that long since had given themselves over to grocery lists, telephone numbers, appointments some kept some broken.

Gleynis' Havana journal:

Morning, coffee: He sleeps. He wakes. I serve rice and beans. He doesn't know what I do with my nights . . . loves being with me at the school. He cherishes a broken toy truck. I don't know where he got it. He bounces a wad of paper, pretending it's a ball. I will buy him a ball for Noel. Fruit, cereal, snacks for him . . . Cigarettes, a makeup case for me . . . Bus transfers. A peso for mami . . . and I leave the light on.

"I think I could like Gleynis. I suppose Marisol is all right too. Dad, are you listening to me?"

"Yes, you said that you like Gleynis."

"What's not to like? She knows you're a writer. Should I tell her what you write about?"

"Sure, why not?

"So . . . what *is* your writing about?"

"I finished a book of short stories last fall. Why don't you take a look at it? I have a copy back at the room."

"Well . . . ?"

"So what do you want to know?"

"So what is it about?"

"Oh, travel mainly. You take a look. How about these notes . . . tell me what you think; "The Charm of the Heart" . . . I got the idea from a story Gleynis told me about a family legend:

The Charm of the Heart

Michael Levi

Great Grandmother Gutierrez, born 1916, married Great Grandfather Andre'.

Abuela Nan, born 1936, married Papi, who was fond of drinking, and not a good farm hand. He disappeared or was disappeared-- no one seems to know.

Gleynis' mami, born 1958. Her husband is a singer in a meringue band, currently appearing in a bar on the outskirts of Havana. The bar is nothing more than a white washed freestanding store, with broken cars and a dog tied to a stick out back.

"That's it?

"That's the story. You need more? Help me with it."

"No thanks, that's between you and Gleynis. I'm sure she can provide you with more titillating information."

Thursday, March 27

Michael kissed his daughter on the cheek and left her to her duties in the school kitchen. The aroma of garlic and plantains frying on a low heat greeted her as she tied a frayed white apron around her waist. There was a faded picture of a jolly chef in a billowy chef's hat on the center of the apron above a dark area where at one time a small pocket might have been stitched. Lillian sang softly as she began her preparations, stacking slices of thinly sliced white bread here, placing pieces of clear wrap there; her eyes followed her father as he disappeared into the eager hands of shouting school children who were thoroughly captivated by him.

Gleynis always arrived at work at least ten minutes before Lillian, and today was no exception. She was already assembling the ingredients to be transformed into sandwiches later. Next she would carefully dole out small amounts of sugary artificial maple syrup that went with the tasty dough she would fry up for breakfast. On occasion an employee or someone from the neighborhood would bring to work a big piece of pork to be equally divided between students and teachers. That was a day than no one wanted to miss. Not all of the children or teachers would get such a great treat on the same day, but over time no one was left out. Such was not the case this day, however. Everyone would have to make due with what could be provided and coated with syrup.

A few days earlier a parent helper brought a red snapper that her brother had caught on a deep-sea fishing trip. That day Gleynis went right to work filleting and baking. She sent Lillian to the store for tomatoes and peppers while she sautéed other vegetables and spices on hand. From these ingredients Gleynis created a sauce to smother the delicacy. The aroma quickly permeated every corner of the school, lifting spirits and bringing with it smiles and bursts of laughter.

"Gleynis let me help . . ."

"Si, gracias . . . here . . . sauté onion, garlic and peppers in olive oil over medium heat while I dice. Do like this, see? We cook it six to eight minutes until becomes tender, not soggy. Then we add tomatoes, tomato paste, bay leaf, capers, olives, wine, salt and pepper."

"Is that all you want me to do?" Lillian asked, playfully sarcastic.

"No, cook the sauce ten minutes more over low to medium heat. After that we add the snapper and cook for about four minutes. Then you flip the fillets and cook for another four minutes. We serve them over white rice and cover with my sauce. Now, did you get all that?"

"Huh?"

Lillian never tired of watching Gleynis prepare food. She admired Gleynis' effortless skill and wanted to emulate it. On one occasion, Gleynis looked up from her work to find Lillian studying her movements. Gleynis smiled and nodded. With a wave of her hand, she encouraged Lillian to resume her work. Embarrassed, Lillian returned her focus on the dirty pots and pans.

"Gleynis how is it you speak English so well?"

"I learned in primary school. One of my teachers was an American, married to a Canadian diplomat. She insisted that her students speak English as their second language."

Lillian nodded. "Well, you're certainly on your way to mastering the language."

Gleynis nodded also.

Later that evening Lillian settled down to write. Relaxing on the balcony with her journal and wine, she was noticed by her neighbors. The children called and waved from their balcony across the way. They laughed and hid when she waved back:

A look of determination on her face, lips tightened, mouth set, Gleynis spreads government peanut butter on bread. Her slender, agile body navigates the kitchen, each utensil an extension of a skilled hand, a . . . surgeon's hand. Dad says Gleynis was a medical student here at the University before she had a child. "How far is the school cafeteria from such an ambition?" I wonder.

Friday, March 28

Wringing out the dishtowel and hanging it over the faucet, Gleynis declared "that's that. Lillian you're coming with me. I want you to meet someone."

"Oh? Where're we going?" Lillian folded her towel in mimicry and deliberately positioned it next to Gleynis'.

"I have to take a few pesos to my mother, and I want to leave Andre' with her for a little bit. Do you think your father will mind if I steal you away? It's not far . . . maybe fifteen minutes . . . no, of course he won't mind," Gleynis said affirmatively, answering her own question.

"No, of course he won't." Lillian was not so sure. "I'll want to tell him where we're going, though."

"Good, first we'll stop off at Marisol's to pick up a few things that she bought me at the market. Then we will go to mami's. You pick up Andre' from his room down the hall on the way back from telling your father. I want to wash up and have a cigarette. I'll meet you on the sidewalk in ten minutes. From there we'll walk to the bus stop. It's not a long ride, and you'll be back at your hotel by early evening."

"Dad, Gleynis asked me to go with her, I think to her mother's. Is that ok?"

"Does she want me to come along?"

"Umm, she didn't mention you, no . . . ."

Marisol was surprised to see that Gleynis had brought Lillian.

"What are you two up to?"

"We're going to mami's."

"I'm coming."

"Suit yourself."

"Mami, this is Lillian. She's from the United States. Her father is Michael Levi, the man I spoke to you about." Gleynis mother took each woman's face in her hands, and in turn, gave them a loud kiss on the cheek. Then she turned to her grandson. "Come here, little papi." Andre' moved toward his grandmother, and winced. " *Dios mio*, you are getting so big, Andre' . . . I love you. Do you love your *abuela*?"

"Si, abuela."

"Gleynis, boil water. Marisol, bring me the tea bags from the cabinet."

"Mami, Lillian's father has a charm that seems to be our Charm. He says he got it from Denis."

"Not possible . . . Our family gave the Charm to Enrique long ago. He did not mention giving it away."

Gleynis turned to Lillian. "Enrique was given a charm, a family keepsake, before he left for Florida. It was meant as a totem, to keep him safe. We call it 'The Charm of the Heart'. Enrique never made it to Florida. He was caught at the 28-mile marker and put in prison. My

144

family assumed The Charm was lost." Then, turning to her mother, "Mami, when you see Enrique, ask him about the Charm."

Gleynis' mother shrugged her shoulders, and then nodded, "If I see him . . ."

"Does the Charm have a special significance to your family?" Lillian asked.

"Mami . . . ?" Gleynis encouraged.

"My mother gave me The Charm when I was fifteen, at the time of my *Quinceanera*, along with my doll . . . The doll is a symbol of childhood that has passed. I wore my mother's dress . . . Marisol, hand me my doll over there." Gleynis' mother leaned forward and pointed to the fireplace mantle, no longer used but for dust and knick-knacks. She continued, "My mother received The Charm from her mother when she was fourteen. The old woman was worried that her daughter was growing too old to marry, so she purchased The Charm from a Santa Rea witch. 'You will now attract a fine husband,' she told my mother. Sure, *The Charm of the Heart*-- that's what the witch called it-- was meant to bring her daughter a husband, but as it turned out, it brought her more than that. It brought her, well, you will just have to come back soon and I will tell you that story." Gleynis' mother smiled, coughed and wheezed a cigarette wheeze, and drank her tea. Gleynis moved in to help her mother, but her mother waved her off and fell back into her chair.

"Mami, you smoke too much. When are you going to quit?"

"When you quit, that's when."

"My family believes that The Charm has power," Gleynis added, turning to Lillian.

"Yes, to some The Charm brings luck, to others; dreams; still others, The Charm brings wisdom," her mother agreed after a long sip.

"It all sounds so . . . superstitious."

"The old ones, Abuela Nan, (sigh) but that was a different time . . . there were so many other forces at work in the world then. Charms and curses were present everywhere. No sooner did a charm show up but a man would disappear. A cow might go dry, and a chicken, well, men and women of great medicine, of a different type than we know of today, walked the earth. We modern women, we have no time to believe, but back then, there was time to believe, to behave in a way that made the miracles of The Charm possible. If Nan were alive, she would tell you children a story or two."

"Your daughter told me that your mother made a gift of The Charm to you for your wedding day. Is that so?"

"She said what? No, of course that is not the way it happened! Get your stories straight, my child," Gleynis' mother replied, feigning hurt and then reaching to hit her daughter with a dog track racing form that was serving time as a coaster to her teacup. "I didn't need a charm to get a man." As she said this, she grabbed Lillian's arm and squeezed it, keeping her hand there for a long moment to show that there were no hard feelings lingering after the comment. Lillian looked into the

146

woman's eyes, and saw a sparkle there. She had seen that sparkle in Gleynis' eyes too.

"Senora Rodriquez, where is The Charm now?"

"I have no idea. As you've heard, I gave the charm to Enrique', but who can tell what he did with it? I haven't seen it since they day he left for Miami. He may very well have given the Charm to his brother, si; otherwise, Enrique would have undoubtedly made it to Miami. *Dios mio.*" She crossed herself, kissed her index and pointer fingers, and offered the kiss to God.

"So you think he might have given it to Denis?"

"No se' . . . as I said, it's possible."

"So you see, Lillian, it could be that your father brought The Charm back to us. For those who believe, it is something that was meant to be . . . your father coming to Havana."

"Well, charm or no charm, I don't think any of us expected to be spending Easter Week in Cuba. This is really one for the books."

Saturday, March 29

"Marisol and I are going to show you two the Havana that only a few privileged citizens have experienced," Gleynis announced as she burst through the entrance to Michael's suite.

"I know Lillian will appreciate that and, by the way, good morning to you too, and thank you for knocking." Michael had been washing and drying dishes, placing the last in the drying rack. The sarcasm was lost on the two young women, as they pushed their way passed him. With her coat slung over one shoulder and exaggerating a hip gyration Marisol approached Michael, winking at him as she careened away just before contact. Gleynis missed the entire scene. Taking a visitor's inventory of the kitchenette, she picked up a dishtowel off the floor and returned it to the rack.

"Lillian, let's get moving. Where are you?" Gleynis slapped Michael on the butt as she left him for the large bedroom beyond. Marisol held back, trying for a better reaction, still accentuating the movement of her hips and looking over one shoulder then the other, Michael pretended not to notice and finished the dishes. Marisol pursed her lips in an exaggerated pout.

"Ok, Marisol, I get it, I get it."

Gleynis knocked on the bathroom door. "Lillian, come on... We don't have all day, *mi hermana*; now hurry up out of there! I have to get in before we leave."

"Day people and night people . . ." Marisol shrugged.

" . . . They are a breed apart, to be sure." Lillian finished Marisol's sentence for her as she emerged from the bathroom and turned the light off.

"Que?"

"I don't know where that came from." Lillian shrugged, exaggerating a gesture of indifference.

"Ladies, let's grab a cab to the other end of town."

"We're fine with the bus, Michael."

"Not today . . . first class."

Gleynis and Marisol took Michael and Lillian on a walking tour of Eastern Havana along the riverfront. First, they stopped for a drink at the Hotel Nacional de Cuba, and while as a rule Cuban citizens are not permitted inside the hotel except on official business, Gleynis and Marisol walked in and were shown to a table in the garden area, with a view of the sea. Michael and Lillian noticed the deference with which their guides were treated. Lillian shot her father a glance but he did not dare acknowledge what his daughter was thinking.

Following drinks, the foursome walked to the former American Embassy, now closed except for limited use as a Cuban Government Administration Building. Barricades surrounded the stark buildings, giving the impression of an Eastern European or Soviet Block compound.

"Lillian, let me show you something." Gleynis grabbed Lillian's arm and led her to the crosswalk. They waited for the light to change and then ran across the street where bulkhead and surf greeted them as old frolicking friends.

Michael waved to them, but the gesture was lost as the two women took off their shoes and disappeared into a staircase leading to a jetty. Soon they were out of sight.

Marisol grabbed Michael's arm, spinning him around.

"So, Miguel, what is it that you want with my Gleynis."

Michael's eyes widened at the question. He had no answer for her. Marisol moved away. She turned and shot Michael a by-now-familiar glance over her shoulder, and without waiting for the light to change, dodged the traffic, disappearing into sea and sand where the two women were waiting.

Sunday, March 30

Michael and Lillian agree to meet Gleynis alone for lunch on Plaza Vieja.

"What's the matter? I can't come?" Marisol asked when Gleynis dropped off Andre'.

"You have your nephew, Flaco, anyway, yes?"

"I wish you would not call him that. He is trying to bulk up. He's sensitive."

"I'm sorry, Marisol."

"That's ok, *mi hermana*, *Si*, I have to mind him," she replied, giving Gleynis a kiss.

Their waiter recognized Gleynis and greeted her warmly. "Michael, this is Jose'. He knows my brother Enrique'. They went to school together. Jose, this is Miguel Levi, and his *hija*, Lilliana."

"*Buenas dias*. Where is Andre'?"

"He is with Marisol. She has her nephew today . . . the perfect play date."

"You're here from the United States?"

"Well, Puerto Rico."

"Juan saw Enrique about a month ago, right here. I thought you'd like to talk with him. Juan, Miguel knows Denis. They met in San Juan."

Lillian, fatigued from the whirlwind of activity that Gleynis had put her through over the past few days, ordered a non-alcoholic iced tea, her eyes opening wide as she studied a small dog yapping at two small boys playing soccer on the cobblestone path in front of the restaurant.

"Miguel, would you like to come inside and see our kitchen facilities. We are proud of them."

"Go ahead, Michael. Lillian and I will be all right for a few minutes."

Michael accepted the waiter's offer, leaving Lillian and Gleynis with the opportunity for girl-talk. At the table to their left, two young women were talking and   smoking while the small child in between them made faces at Lillian and Gleynis. To their right an elderly man had finished his meal, and a waiter brought him an espresso. He returned Lillian's glance as if he were about to say something. "Lillian, what're your impressions of Havana so far? Do you think that you'd be able to live here for an extended period of time?"

"It truly is beautiful here."

"Do you have a boyfriend at home?"

"I was seeing someone, but no, not now, no boyfriend."

"How long did you know him, before you, you know . . . ?"

"I didn't, 'you know '."

"Did he realize how much you cared for him?"

"Actually, we didn't communicate all that much. I'm not even sure if I liked him a whole lot. Why do you ask?"

"No reason . . . just a wonder." Gleynis lit another cigarette.

Michael returned by himself, the check apparently paid. "Let's go, ladies."

"Michael, thank you . . . I have to pick up Andre."

"Can I walk you? Call you a cab?"

"No, thank you. I'll walk to the bus from here. See you both tomorrow."

Michael and Lillian returned to their hotel, with no definite plan beyond relaxing and a walk to the Piazza. "Dad, what was all that waiter business about?"

"Enrique was working in the kitchen."

"You're kidding! Why didn't you bring him out to say hello?"

"I couldn't. He's in hiding."

"You mean from a legal standpoint?"

"Not really. It depends on how you look at it. He's working as a dishwasher. He still runs his wheelbarrows, but secretly supplements his income."

"Damn, did he say anything else?"

"Watch your language, Lillian." Then, "Yes. He asked about his brother, and wanted to know if Denis ever mentioned The Charm of The Heart."

"Wow, well, why would he ask that?"

"*No se'.*"

"Well did he tell you anything else?"

"He told me that he did not believe in the Charm before he left Cuba, but that he had given it to Denis that night on the beach anyway:"

"Here, little brother, take this. You will need it and more to get where we are going."

"Enrique was among the first to be captured, along with some of his uncles, aunts, cousins and friends at the 28-mile marker. He returned to Havana and put in prison for more than a year. I know the rest of the story from listening to Denis. He escaped in a different boat. The Cuban Navy fired upon them and everyone was killed except him. Denis was wounded but managed to hide under the bodies as his boat drifted in the Gulf Stream. Eventually he was picked up by a tanker bound for the Gulf of Mexico, and found his way to relatives in Miami."

"How did Denis wind up in Puerto Rico?"

"He worked his way through school in Miami, in the restaurant business; first as a dish washer, then busboy and waiter, then shift manager. When a full manager's spot opened up in San Juan, he grabbed it. Eventually he saved enough money to put a down payment on *Moorings*. The rest you know . . ."

Monday, March 31

"Por favor, Senorita." The young mother motioned to Lillian to follow her as she and her son passed through the door of the grocery where Lillian bought the treats for the students. A tiny bell announced their arrival. As the three entered, she grabbed Lillian by the arm and pointed in the direction of the diaper packages behind the cash register on the old wooden counter. Lillian took a few pesos from her purse and handed them to the cashier, wondering if they were enough to purchase what the woman needed. She exited the store hastily, not wanting to lose track of her father.

Finding her father waiting for her, Lillian put her arm in his and began to walk away. He stood fast and pulled her back, pointing through the store window to where she had just made her purchase.

"C'mon, Dad, we will be late for school."

"Wait. Look there, Lil," he insisted, grabbing her arm and pointing through the store window.

Together they watched as the young woman pushed the package of diapers back across the counter. The cashier took Lillian's money out of the cash register, handing a portion to the young mother, while placing the remainder of it in the pocket of her smock. The two women nodded and spoke a few words to one another.

A look of surprise came over Lillian's face. She laughed at her own gullibility as the mother and son scam artists opened the door. The tiny bell announced their departure.

Brushing past Lillian without even noticing that she was glaring at them, the two thieves walked back the way they had come. The mother's hand clasped firmly around her son's arm as she hurried him along, she was on the lookout for their next shopping victim.

"Dad, the breakfasts are great," Lillian said as she got up from her table to get herself more water melon and kiwi-- her favorites.

Michael guessed he was paying more than his share for the "free" breakfasts through inflated hotel room rates. Whatever the cost though, Lillian was right. The meals were always freshly prepared and served hot. And you couldn't beat the conversation. Michael and Lillian would take their time, greeting new visitors who after a few days seemed like old friends.

Tuesday, April 1

Lillian's Havana journal:

I love the time I spend with dad-- especially our breakfast hour. Dad can't stop talking and sometimes he just sits there and laughs. Our work at the Jose' Machado school has made this visit even more special. I can easily stay here for as long as this is going to last. I wonder if that is what Gleynis meant when she asked me those questions in the park the other day. On our morning walks, we look for new restaurants as we explore every side street and alley. We read the menus posted in tiny restaurant windows and doorways. The star-shaped layout of the ancient streets give up their secrets and just as quickly hid familiar pathways again:

"Dad, I think we've been here before."

"Lillian, I think we've been everywhere before."

Old Havana is a town of convenience rather than geometry and economics. Just when we're sure we've discovered a short cut from one place to another, our destination goes missing again! The food is home-style, delicious, and inexpensive. There are so many herbs and spices used in the cooking; I cannot discern them all. My taste buds just can't keep up with the onslaught of so many tasty delights! I am going to have to ask Gleynis to show me how to prepare food the way the Cubans do . . .

Dad and I traveled by coco taxi to parts of the city that were farther away from the hotel than a twenty-minute walk. These quaint vehicles, little more than Vespa scooters with fiberglass shells over the rear axle, allowed just enough room for two passengers, offering scant weather protection or relief from choking traffic emissions. My extremely loyal father prefers to use the same driver each time. Unfortunately, the driver displays the same loyalty and always shows up with the same vehicle. His oil- stained, poor excuse for a taxi has a bad clutch, no muffler or other air pollution device, and more often than not, little breaking ability.

Wednesday, April 2

The air grew warmer, the days seemed brighter and the sky cloudless, except for the predictable evening shower that rumbled in from the north every late afternoon. "Lillian, no visit to Havana would be complete without a trip to the University." Michael and Lillian found their driver, Felix, waiting for them by the sidewalk.

"I don't remember you calling Felix," Lillian whispered from the back seat.

"No need to. I told him to stop by each day this week around twelve, just in case we need him," Michael's voice a whisper also. Lillian could not hear her father above the grinding of the clutch.

"*Eso no un problema, senor*, either way . . ." Felix shouted from the driver's seat.

"Why don't we just take another cab, Dad?" Lillian turned to her father, ignoring the driver's comment.

"In Havana, Lillian, as with any trip away from home, it's a good thing to find someone you can rely on, even if that level of reliability might not extend to the transportation at hand."

The conversation ended there. Lillian shook her head in disbelief. She would have to be content to watch the sidewalks and storefronts whiz past as the coco taxi sped along the bumpy Havana streets; streets in dire need of repair.

The University of Havana was located in the epicenter of downtown Havana, on Calle San Lázaro. Felix parked at the base of a large staircase, along the busy thoroughfare.

As Michael, Lillian, and Felix climbed the long steps leading to a grassy mall area, a student in his early twenties approached. Judging by the way the student greeted Felix; it seemed they knew each other.

"Juan, these are two friends of mine from the United States, Michael and Lillian Levi," Felix said in Spanish, offering his right hand to the student and extending his left arm to Juan's shoulder for a display of camaraderie.

Lillian extended her hand without hesitation. Her father did the same.

"How much does it cost to go to school here?" Lillian asked.

"There is no cost, Senorita," Juan replied. "All students attend free," he said with pride, "provided they pass the entrance exams."

"Are students permitted to leave Cuba after they graduate?"

"A graduate may apply, but must wait five years after graduation to be considered. Once a request is made to leave, the law degree or the medical degree is suspended until emigration is complete. Most graduates that fill out the paperwork actually never leave. What would be the point, after all that education, Senorita? It's an honor for most to remain in Cuba following graduation, or the student would not have worked so hard to graduate."

Felix fell silent, looking at Michael. Michael looked at Lillian; a look that said, "No more questions."

Juan pointed to a large building to Lillian's left, framing part of the common grassy mall area. He spoke reverently of the classroom where Fidel Castro studied to become an attorney. Michael listened intently as this story was told, and Lillian told her father later that in her opinion happening upon Juan was not an accident.

"It all seemed a bit too scripted," Lillian said.

"So you will have a good story to tell when you return home."

As their tour came to an end, Michael offered the student two pesos for the tour information. Juan glanced around nervously.

"Michael, Cubans may not accept money from outsiders," Felix said. "However, I will give Juan a peso later from my taxi money, if that's your wish."

Ready for a mid-day meal, Felix recommended a *paladar* a few blocks from the University.

"*Paladar*?" Lillian asked.

"*Si*. A *paladar* is a restaurant operated in the proprietor's home," Felix began as they walked down the steps and back to their little vehicle. "Generally these small enterprises are run "off-the-radar". While they are not officially approved of, the paladar is unofficially tolerated, most likely because they offer up some of the most delicious food on the island. Everyone eats at one, sooner or later."

Felix skillfully guided their buggy to a narrow residential side street. Michael and Lillian stepped onto the sidewalk. There was nothing unusual about the area; a mixture of residential buildings that had not seen renovation since the nineteen fifties, or before.

There were a few store fronts but this was not a commercial district. Laundry lines dangled from tiny second, third and fourth floor balconies; balconies showing off flowers and vegetables in planters of every size. There were kitchen chairs and small kitchen tables where family members were eating, calling to nearby neighbors, and playing cards, checkers or dominoes.

Felix approached the door close to where he parked. He knocked and jiggled the door latch. A man appeared, looked up and down the street, then nodded and ushered the patrons across the threshhold. The man once again looked up and down the street before stepping inside the breezeway, closing and locking the door behind him. He nodded to Felix as he greeted each of them individually.

Lillian hesitated as her eyes got used to the dark foyer. She was usheredby her father toward the staircase as Felix turned to leave.. Michael said, "Wait a minute, Felix . . . join us . . . my treat." They all moved quickly up the first set of stairs.

At the first landing, Lillian turned to her father for assurance. He gestured to continue along the hallway at the top of the landing. Turning a sharp, dimly lit corner, they entered an apartment. Continuing through a series of little rooms they came to what may have been at one time a main living area with large windows that faced the street. There were a number of tables set with tablecloths and place settings. Once seated, hand-written menus with limited fare were

162

brought along with bottled water. A waitress and a bus boy stood by, eager to please the patrons.

"Senor Levi, excuse me. I'm going to wash my hands. I'll be right back."

When Felix was gone, Lillian asked, "Dad, why did you move to Puerto Rico?"

"I was dissatisfied with my job . . . bored with my life." Michael took a sip of water, swishing before he swallowed. Looking out the window, his attention was drawn to a balcony across the way. A small child was corralled precariously in a makeshift playpen, occupying herself with a small doll. "Do you see that . . . ?"

Lillian broke in. Now that she had him, she was going to hang on. "And while we are on the subject of you, what is the significance of *The Man with the Butterfly Tattoo* . . . ?" She fumbled in her purse for a journal and bits of paper.

Michael darkened. "It was a poem I'd written for a friend when I was back in Jersey. It could have been part of something more elaborate. At one time I thought I had something there, but I haven't worked on it for some time. Let's leave it there for now.

"Are you referring to the writing or the subject of the piece?"

"If I have time I will pick it up again," Michael said, ignoring her comment, "but if I don't, maybe you'll work on it sometime, huh?"

"So there *is* some meaning attached to these writings. Michael Levi, *man of mystery*," Lillian said, tinkling the ice in her glass and giving her father an exaggerated wink.

"As I said, it might be a part of something more significant later, if I'm of a mind to work on it."

Michael took his journal from his pocket. He opened to a page he had marked with a sticky note, offering the book across the table. "You want to read something . . . read this. This is what I've been working on the last couple days . . . part of it is from a recent dream."

Lillian read aloud:

"I looked everywhere for her in my life, even though I knew then that she would never return. I called to her in my dreams. There was no reply. I hoped for her to the end of hope, on the chance she was waiting even there . . .

. . . one day long after I had given up, there was a tap on my left shoulder and she was standing next to me. I turned and opened my eyes wide to drink her in; I filled my eyes with the sight of her. Tears of joy enveloped me . . ."

"Did you say, 'The left shoulder'?" Lillian paused.

"There are those that say that Death Himself taps on the left shoulder."

Lillian paused for a long moment and looked up. Her father was looking at her. He was listening to her every word, as if she was the author of what was being read and he was hearing it for the first time. She continued:

" . . . In my dream I entered a room full of people. She was sitting on a stool, a glass in her hand, not looking in my direction. I approached and she turned to me. Without speaking, she extended

164

her hand and placed a small charm, a heart-shaped charm , into my

shirt pocket. At once a sensation of contentment washed over me, and

I awoke with those same feelings. I held on to that sense of pleasure

and peace until the sensation slowly vanished, as dream feelings tend

to disappear during the course of the day.

"Dad, that story reminds me of Denis Rodriguez. Did you ever show this journal to him?"

"Not that I remember. It's just a story. Anyway, that's not the end of it."

"You mean this woman returned to you?"

"Yes, well not exactly . . ."

"So . . . ?"

Michael did not answer her.

"You know, Dad, you could never keep a good woman, not even in your dreams. So who is this woman and how is it that she has taken you away from your family?"

"Thanks a lot, daughter. Seriously , I don't think it's a person . . . more a feeling that comes and goes in dreams. I never really had her in the first place, and I think that may be the point. I gained nothing, lost nothing. Honey, let's order. I'm hungry. I want to get back to the hotel and walk a bit."

"That sounds good. Dad, I want to tell you something. Thanks for inviting me here."

"Did I?" Michael finished his water. Lillian chewed on her lemon slice and jingled her ice. She watched the bus boy as he approached their table. Cancun came to mind.

"Senor, Felix asked me to tell you that he would wait for you outside. He wanted to check the oil in the taxi." Michael nodded, grateful for the opportunity to have spoken to his daughter alone.

The longer Lillian was with her father, the more comfortable she grew with their renewed relationship, and with her surroundings. The allure of the ancient colonial cityscape and the sense of reconnecting with family combined deepened and renewed her spirit. She thought less and less of existence back home. Lillian was content just being her father's daughter, in his charge, in this magical place. The everyday actions of walking and talking took on a mystical quality in Havana, and Lillian viewed these everyday events with new eyes.

"Café con leche?" the owner of the establishment came to their table.

"Yes, please," Michael smiled. Lillian nodded.

The woman returned with coffee and a special fruity, flaky pastry. Father and daughter never knew if the desert had been added to the bill, but neither cared. The ride home in the coco taxi was a delight; the end of a perfect Havana afternoon that both would remember, dream about, and write about in a variety of ways for the rest of their lives.

Thursday, April 3

"What do you think your brothers are up to today?"

Lillian stopped mid-butter knife-to-toast transfer. "Oh my goodness, yes, Jack and Dashell . . . I was supposed to get in touch with them. I'd better send an email today . . . and mom too. How can we do that?"

"*No problema, hija*. We can head back to the center of Old Havana today right after work, and you can use the computer where we had dinner a few nights ago. Does that work for you?"

"Great! Dad, I want to talk to you about Gleynis."

"I'm all talked out, Lil. Why don't we get going? We have a long day ahead."

Friday, April 4

Lillian's Havana journal:

Dad's not well. His writing makes little sense, and although he believes he is on to something with his dreams and visions, it all adds up to a bunch of nothing. He needs to give himself a little distance from Gleynis. She only clouds the situation. What's he hoping to gain there anyway? . . . And Gleynis . . . ? Gleynis . . . .

Saturday, April 5

Gleynis' Havana journal:

I've been thinking about Lillian. Why would she travel this far to find her father? Michael would undoubtedly return to his family sooner or later. I know men, and I know this man. He will be leaving Cuba soon. Ultimately, there would be nothing for him here . . .

On the other hand, there is more on this man's mind than this vacation, his work, or even his family. I am going to ask Marisol what she thinks . . .

Paving repairs were taking place on each street in the old part of the city. Asphalt would be costly even if it was available, but bricks were abundant and made inexpensively from the clay along the banks of the Almendares River near the town of Tapaste, where the waters are shallow and the silt heavy. Day laborers were busy everywhere, disrupting tourist routes with street improvement projects at almost every turn of the narrow streets. There were no direct routes anywhere in Old Havana, making second-guessing the construction sites all the more perplexing.

Up one narrow one-way street and down another the coco taxi traveled. Felix' singing could be heard above the grinding clutch and its muffler-less engine. Skillfully skirting a barricade covering a series of drainage ditches then deftly completing a reverse maneuver, he avoided a donkey cart full of bricks and straw.

Lillian eyed the progress as the coco taxi passed each work site. Tourists trampled the manual grades the workmen had set just moments before.

"Hey, watch out over there! Get back here and fix that!" Lillian shouted. The bricklayers and stonemasons didn't mind the numerous footprints, however. They repaired their work as required, and continued on with their labor.

"Why don't the men put up more barricades, Dad?"

"It gives them something to do all day. The work eventually gets done, and have you noticed the remarkable level of craftsmanship when a portion of the street is finished? I would bet the workers welcome the attention paid them by tourists, and the opportunity the tradesmen are given to show off their expertise. Take a look at the antique tools being used to set those grades. No modern levels and transits here. A few hammers, a twelve-foot-long two-by-four, and a supply- laden donkey standing by for when materials are needed. That's all."

"Thanks, o' my tour guide," Lillian squeezed his arm hard and went back to watching the action on the street.

Sunday, April 6

Michael and Lillian dressed and prepared to leave the hotel for *Hemingway's* where they were to meet Gleynis for dinner. It would be Lillian's last night in Havana. She was flying back to Cancun on Monday morning. Lillian still had one more question for Gleynis: "Does she know my father is not well?"

"Do you want me to call Felix, Lil?" Michael asked when they stepped outside their hotel.

"No *thank* you. I want to live to remember our last night together with two feet on the ground, not on three wheels or less."

Gleynis was seated at a table when Michael and Lillian arrived. She didn't stand when they joined her, but tinkled her empty mojito glass at the waitress. The three spoke little during the meal. Michael's relationship with Gleynis had deteriorated over the past week. Michael pushed for something that wasn't in the cards. Gleynis pushed back not knowing at what.

As the three were finishing dinner, a special announcement flashed across the TV in the bar. The program was in Spanish with no subtitles, so Gleynis translated: "Raul Castro announced today that cell phones are now permissible for citizens' use on the island of Cuba." With that announcement the patrons cheered and waved at the television set. Many reached into their pockets, purses and packs to proudly show off the cell phones that they already purchased and kept hidden. Waving them in the air many patrons called out, "Viva Raul!" while others shouted, "Viva, Fidel" There was then a chant among the clientele at the bar: "Che'! Che'!, Che'!, Che'! . . . " The bartender set up a round of shot glasses and filled each with tequila. These were passed out at the bar. Then the waitresses worked the tables to see if the dinner patrons would like to join in on the toast to their leaders. Lillian noticed that almost everyone ordered a drink.

As dessert was being served, Lillian reached over and impulsively embraced Gleynis, who allowed this display of affection but did not return the gesture. Lillian held onto the hug a moment longer, and then released her grip. She whispered something to Gleynis before releasing her. Gleynis whispered something in return.

Looking up from his banana cream pie, Michael caught the embrace but said nothing and took another bite, blushing when he realized he intruded on a private moment.

Lillian composed herself and sampled her pie, washing it down with a sip of coffee without looking up. Michael did not notice the tears in his daughter's eyes.

Two years later, Lillian would place this scene into the forward of her first novel, Sealed with a Kiss : *A Caribbean Journey*:

In the spring of 2008 I traveled to Puerto Rico with my   brothers to visit my father, Michael Levi.   Learning that he already left on holiday, I flew to Cancun, Mexico, and finally to Havana, Cuba. There I found him staying at the Hotel Tejadillo, in the part of the city known as Habana Vieja, or 'Old Havana'.   While in Havana my father had taken up company with Gleynis Gutierrez Rodriguez, a cook at a local elementary school.   This is the story of my brief visit to Havana, where I spent two weeks with my father and his unlikely companion.

Lillian's Havana journal:

By the time of our last dinner together Michael *and Gleynis were hardly speaking. Encouraging words from me here and there couldn't melt the iceberg that had formed between them.*

My father had unfinished business with Gleynis, as she did with him, but neither was willing to make the first move. By this time, I understood that my father would have loved to take Gleynis back to Puerto Rico with him, thereby reuniting her with her brother, Denis. I also sensed that she might have been willing to go if it were possible, but at what cost? First, there was Andre' to consider. If Gleynis remained in Cuba, at least she had a job; one where she was able to provide for and protect her son. Yes, I could have influenced the outcome of our final evening together using a daughter's body language and a girlfriend's eye contact.

At one point in the evening, I whispered to Gleynis, "Girl, I love your top." She replied, "Gracias, it's yours."

Lillian excused herself from the dinner table and moved to a seat at the bar. She ordered another drink and struck up a conversation with a member of the band as he readied his guitars on the tiny bandstand near the front window. "There are so many broken hearts to gather," Lillian thought as she looked across the room to her father and Gleynis. "Where is my journal when I need it?" The voice in her head trailed off

174

as she returned to her drink, the tuning of the instruments carrying her away.

Lillian's move gave Michael and Gleynis the opportunity to confront each other one last time before Michael would finalize his plans with the airline. Gleynis offered her frank evaluation of her relationship with Michael. As Lillian looked in their direction, she could tell that they were arguing:

". . . and Michael, you are one selfish son of a bitch. You think only of yourself. You forget that I have a son. What happens to me does not matter as much as what happens to Andre'. When you are ready to face that fact, then we can talk. Otherwise, we have nothing left to say to each other."

The music started, and Lillian looked again in the direction of the table from where she had come. Her father looked unhappy. He was sitting still, and appeared to be listening. Gleynis was animated, her hand gestures broadcasting the nature of the conversation.

"Look at my dad. What does he think he is going to get out of all this? And Gleynis, younger than me even, giving him his due," Lillian laughed to herself, guzzling down her drink faster than was good for her. Lillian stopped laughing. As she sat on her bar stool, fixated on the conversation that she could see but not hear, she thought of Gleynis' obligation to Andre'. She wondered what it would be like to have a son who would not grow up to experience the freedoms that she, Lillian, took for granted. "How far would Gleynis go to insure Andre's freedom?" she wondered.

After the first set, Lillian returned to the table. Michael looked sheepish as Gleynis became quiet. She lit a cigarette, took a deep drag, and looked away. Michael excused himself from the table. Lillian thought her father was going to use the bathroom, but he walked briskly to the door and stepped outside.

"I know that your father is not well, Lillian. Has he spoken to you about this?" Gleynis asked bluntly.

"Well, no," Lillian replied, taken by surprise. "Actually, it was your brother, Denis, who told me. My father has not said more than a word or two about his health."

"Still, a woman knows, yes? A woman knows her man as well as a daughter knows her father."

Lillian realized then that it did not matter what Gleynis knew. The only important question was, "does Gleynis love my father?"

"I admit that I'm jealous of my father's feelings for you. Can you understand that?"

"Of course I do. Can you understand that I hate putting your father off? Here is a man that doesn't know his mind. Perhaps I don't know mine, either. On the other hand, I have a child to think of, and that consideration comes before all others."

"Well, maybe you're not giving my father enough credit. He may be able to help you."

"Maybe so, but it seems he can't help himself."

Lillian felt an uncontrollable emotion well inside of her, but she blinked back her tears. Naturally Gleynis did not show any such emotion; she would forever be an angelic statue that had fallen off the cathedral wall during a summer shower in the otherwise sunny life of the Levi family.

"Lillian, I have something for you." Gleynis reached into her purse and pulled out a simple silver chain. "Here. My mother asked me to give this to you. I believe it once held a heart-shaped charm . . . maybe even *the* Charm. Lillian allowed Gleynis to fasten it around her neck.

"Thank you, Gleynis. Thank your mother too. It's beautiful.

Meanwhile Michael composed himself outside and returned to the table. By the time the check arrived he, Gleynis, and Lillian, each in their way, were worn-out and speechless, equally set in their own resolve. They walked the distance back to the hotel in silence; the only sound their footfall on the moist brick pavement.

Arriving at the hotel, Lillian yawned. "I need to get to bed early. "Tomorrow will be a long day that will begin before the sun rises." She was wondering what her pool boy was up to in Cancun. She kissed her father goodnight and hugged Gleynis goodbye.

"Goodnight, Dad." Lillian hugged her father a second time, and gave Gleynis a long look.

"Don't be too late if you're going with me to the airport in the morning."

Looking deeper into Gleynis' eyes, Lillian thought, "They really are beautiful. My father has spoken of them on more than one occasion, but until now . . ." then, into Gleynis' ear she whispered, "A daughter knows her father."

Michael gestured to the hotel desk clerk to call Gleynis a taxi.

"A drink before we say our good byes?" he asked Gleynis.

"Maybe I'll wait for the cab here."

"Suit yourself."

Michael walked across the hotel lobby and into the bar. Gleynis stood there with her hands on her hips. Reaching for a cigarette, she stopped for a moment. With the pack back in her purse she followed the direction Michael had taken. He was already sitting at the bar when she entered. The bartender brought two shots of tequila and set them both in front of Michael. When he saw that Gleynis had followed him, Michael slid one shot in front of the adjacent stool.

"Gleynis, it's time that I returned to San Juan," Michael said, drinking his shot. Gleynis' eyes sparkling drank her shot without hesitation.

"So you have said on more than one occasion."

"Well, it is obvious that . . . ."

"Dios mio, Miquel, my grandmother would have taken a strap to you."

Gleynis' Havana Journal:

I was upset not so much with Michael, but with Lillian. I could not remember when I was so out of control with my emotions. Imagine, fighting over a man with his daughter! Of course I can't stay mad at her. I could never harbor any harsh feelings toward her. In many ways we are alike . . . we have gain and loss in common between us. I have been told that I am not a possessive woman. Besides, in the long run Andre' and I are more than Michael, or any man, can handle.

Monday, April 7

"So Dad, you're not coming with me?' Lillian asked as she placed her personal items into her overnight bag.

"I'll take a flight later in the week. I need at least one more day. Besides, you need to get home to put some order back in your life. Your job is waiting, and for sure someone is waiting."

"Ok, I love you. No more coco taxis, though. Call me a real cab this time, ok?"

"I already called you one, first class." Just then a horn honked twice. Michael peered over the balcony and looked down, straining to see around the corner on to Calle' Tejadillo.

"See, it's already outside and waiting." Michael's forced cheerfulness did not fool his daughter.

"Love you, *Michael,*" Lillian emphasized. Dad, this has been such a great trip, really, thank you so much for suggesting . . . ."

". . . my pleasure, daughter. Here, I want you to have this. It will get you home safely. Michael reached into his pocket and handed her the heart-shaped charm that Denis had given him.

"Dad, is this the one that all the fuss is about? Is this the Charm of the Heart?"

"I don't know about that, but it seemed to be an object of great importance to Denis"

Lillian turned it over in her hand.

" . . . Denis gave me that right before I left for Cancun. He said it would bring me luck. I suppose it did. It brought me you. I hope that it'll do the same for you one day."

To Lillian's surprise, Felix was her driver.

"Senorita, I thought you would be more comfortable."

"Why didn't you think of my comfort two weeks ago? Bye, Dad, I love you."

Michael waved goodbye as a group of school children ran up the street, kicking a new soccer ball that Lillian had given them.

"Has it only been two weeks since I left Cancun?" Lillian drew back the heavy drapes on a late Caribbean afternoon. Fingering the Charm in her pocket, she pulled the second layer of translucent curtains aside, opened the sliding door, and stepped onto her balcony. A pre-wedding party was getting started poolside below, the mood of which was spreading across the pool area to the southeastern end of the complex where surf, sand, and man-made paradise came together to create a surreal ambiance.

The sun dropped out of sight behind the hotel to the west, casting long shadows over the poolside cabanas and tiki bars that stood sentry behind the legion of chaise lounges. From her balcony chaise, Lillian silently toasted the bride and groom, indistinguishable among billowy summer dresses and crisp sport jackets. Enjoying a Vodka Collins that she mixed from the wet bar in her room, Lillian leaned back, closed her eyes and listened as the party conversation mingled with surf and wind. Wait staff made vain attempts to hold the starched tablecloths in place, as dresses billowed like sails and the Caribbean wind worked its way through the gathering revelers. Sterno fires were bullied by the wind faster than poolside help could relight them. Flowered centerpieces toppled into the lush growth along the walkways.

Peacocks were roaming about just as they did two weeks before, leaving excrement and haunting echoes in their wake. This time Lillian listened for their call with anticipation rather than annoyance. Turning her head to the adjacent balcony and opening her eyes, it was evident that the college co-eds were gone. Judging by the out-of-date bathing suits hung over the railing and the beach toys stacked on a side table, the girls had been replaced by an older couple. Perhaps they had brought a grandchild

The taste of sea salt that gathered in the back of her throat added to Lillian's sense of exhilaration and exhaustion, yet she did not want to sleep. On the ride out to the sand bar from the airport, she had noticed the *Margaritaville Bar and Restaurant* just minutes from her hotel. At this memory Lillian snapped her fingers, jumped up, and began preparing for the evening. Before dressing, she applied lotion to her dry skin. The weeks of Caribbean wind and water had dried her out completely. Lillian paused nude in front of her dresser mirror. She posed with her hands on her hips, her eyes taking inventory over an imperfect body; a little scar on her lower left leg from a childhood bicycle accident, an ankle bracelet lived there now, all but concealing it.

Taking the Charm of the Heart from her small bag, she carefully strung it onto the silver necklace that Gleynis had given her. She then clasped the totem around her neck.

"A quick bite and a tropical drink would be a great way to end my last evening in Cancun," Lillian thought. Not remembering how far the restaurant was from the hotel, she asked the bell captain to call her a taxi.

"That's not a problem, Miss. Please take the first one in line down there," he replied, pointing to the circular drive beneath the hotel portico. "Walk outside, down the steps to the driveway, and to the right."

"Thank you," Lillian handed the bell captain two dollars, and left the lobby.

"Where to, Miss?" the driver asked as he opened the rear door for her. Instinctively she headed for the passenger seat.

"You'll be more comfortable here," he said, pointing the way to the seat as he opened the rear door.

"Yes, thank you . . . Margaritaville, please."

The driver closed the door, crushing his cigarette before getting behind the wheel.

The cab turned right out of the drive and traveled north for five or six blocks until it came to a u-turn. Lillian noticed that the driver could have turned south as he exited the hotel, but she guessed that he was just making his fare. The restaurant was actually only three blocks south of the Hyatt Caribe'; an easy walk.

Lillian checked with the hostess but all tables were taken. She left her name and went to the bar. Manuel was there, watching the giant screen as Jimmy Buffet and his band played on a beach somewhere outdoors in a tropical setting.

"Hi, Manuel, how are you? Beer, please." Lillian nodded and climbed onto the stool next to him.

"Senorita, welcome back . . . how was your trip?"

"Great, thanks . . . my name is Lillian."

The two exchanged pleasantries, but as her father asked, she did not discuss where she had been. "That's a beautiful necklace and charm. Did you buy them on your trip?"

"Yes, no . . . my father gave me the charm. A friend gave me the chain."

"The other one, the pukka shells, I picked up at the hotel." Lillian decided not to pursue her friendship with Manuel any further. She ordered another beer and shared her food with him. He asked if she would like to join him at a table. "You know what? I think I'll just enjoy the evening from here. Thanks anyway." A few minutes later, the hostess came into the bar and called her name. Lillian waved her off. The waitress shrugged and walked away, calling the name of the next fortunate group of *parrot heads*.

"So many broken hearts to gather," Lillian said under her breath.

"You were saying . . . ?" Manuel asked, his attention taken away from the big screen.

"You said that to me on the beach a few weeks ago. Do you remember?"

"I'm sorry, no, I don't."

"Maybe not . . ." Lillian could not remember where or when she had heard the words that flew in and out of her mind like a colorful kite without a string. Jimmy Buffett and the Corral Reefer Band were now playing the hit, "Volcano" on the big screen. Suddenly a ten-foot tall paper mache mountain in the corner of the bar erupted during the last verse, rumbling from inside its textured cliffs as it spewed theatrical smoke. That was Lillian's cue. Saying goodnight, she paid her tab and Manuel's. She checked her watch: 11:47. It was such a beautiful night, and remembering that her hotel was just three blocks away, she decided to walk home.

Manuel escorted her to the door. His eyes followed her as she strolled up the drive and turned onto the sidewalk swinging her small beach bag into a secure place over her shoulder. She was met by a strong westward wind as she moved along, her hair a kitten-and-string tangle. She stopped to take a deep breath, allowing the ocean spray and night air to penetrate her lungs. Closing her eyes Lillian thought of Gleynis. She could smell the memory of Gleynis in the breeze that traveled over the sandy dunes. Lillian missed her new friend. The squinty starlight brightness of the street lamps lining Boulevard Kulkulcan cast their spell, beckoning Lillian back to the Malecon. She began to cry. Tears flowed like acid-rain drips from the saints-in-relief on the Cathedral Walls of Old Havana.

Back at the hotel, she lingered outside in the circular drive, looking at the stars until her tears were under control. Entering the front door, Lillian walked directly through the lobby to the pool area. She expected to find activity there, but it was too late. The cleaning crew was already vacuuming the pools and hosing down sidewalks in preparation for the next Cancun morning sunrise. Lillian returned to her room, clicked on the news, and took off her clothes. She climbed into bed with her journal by her side, but made no entry on this night. She was asleep before the pen hit the floor.

Tuesday, April 8

Lillian woke before dawn eager to repeat her Cancun morning ritual. Securing the curtains and opening the sliding door, her senses were again hit by the full impact of the emerging Caribbean morning. It was not yet sunrise. On this Tuesday morning even the peacocks were still asleep.

The pool below beaconed with a hypnotic, shimmering light. Straining her neck, she turned her gaze toward the bridge, hoping to spot the figure of the man who had caught her attention weeks ago. Disappointed that he was not there, Lillian looked back into her hotel room toward the bedside table to check the time, but the clock was not in its usual place.

" . . . I must have knocked it over in my sleep." Dressing in shorts, t-shirt and sandals, she rode the elevator to the lobby. "I've got to catch one more sunrise," she told a maid who began moving her cleaning supplies into the elevator before Lillian had a chance to step into the lobby. Lillian hesitated for a moment before excusing herself while sidestepping the bucket and mop.

The maid, a short dark-skinned woman, smiled, embarrassed.

"I'm sorry, miss."

"It's ok. Have a nice day."

Manuel was already in the patio area, skimming the overnight accumulation of insects and leaves. He was singing quietly as he performed his morning duties:

"Para bailar La Bamba, Para bailar La Bamba, Se necessita ua poca de gracia."

Hearing the song, Lillian was reminded of her first dinner with her father, Gleynis and Marisol. She greeted Manuel as she caught the tune in mid-air and downloaded it permanently into her head. This time it was she who said, "mira", pointing toward the horizon beyond the churning ocean. And she was not alone: there were other guests waiting for the sunrise experience; sea and sky did not disappoint. The earth's rotation gave birth to another dawn, captivating all present. A morning hymn of, "Ooh" and "Ah," rose to the heavens above.

Within seconds the day had made its presence fully known, and the magic of the moment was over and done, locked away with the pool vacuums for another twenty-four hours. Employees once again moved about, preparing for the onslaught tourists who were not yet awake; the tourists who, in their morning reverie, could not have imagined the birth that was witnessed just an hour before as they snuggled new lovers, stumbled into showers, squeezed toothpaste and slathered shaving cream.

Breakfast carts were being wheeled about, juice glasses upturned. Napkins were folded and put in their places, just to the right of breakfast plates and bowls. Tablecloths awaited toast crumbs and freshly liberated crayons of the Cancun Holiday tourist season.

188

Everything made sense to the predictable tourists in this safe and unadventurous vacation spot. An excited child darted out of the elevator the moment the door opened, chased after by his nervous parents. "Now don't get near that pool, Sydney . . ."

Most hotel guests were awake only if they needed to catch a tour bus or a flight.

"Day people and night people," Lillian sighed again before entering the elevator. "They are indeed a breed apart."

Lillian returned to New Jersey by way of Charlotte, North Carolina, and while she was concerned that she would be questioned at immigration about her jaunt to Cuba, the agent did not examine her papers closely. He was more interested in whether the person appearing before him was actually the person named on the passport.

"What do you do here in the States?" the uniformed man asked, casually flipping the pages of her passport.

"I write."

"And what do you write, Miss . . . Levi?"

"Oh, you know . . . what does anybody?" Lillian replied, tired and at once impatient. Then she caught herself. "Sorry."

"Welcome home." The uniformed man showed no further interest or curiosity in the arriver's lurid past. Stamping Lillian's paperwork to document her entry, he simply nodded while summoning the next person in line.

Four: Michael

Monday, April 7

Michael watched the taxi pull away from the curb. He waved goodbye but the vehicle was already around the corner where Calle' Tejadillo meets the Malecon, and out of sight.

It was time to make plans for his return to San Juan. Michael emailed his real estate agent and asked her to keep a lookout for "a two bedroom floor plan". He considered buying a plane ticket on line, but changed his mind and decided that he would get one at the airport. The flights to Cancun were never full.

"Why the change . . . ?" Luz Gomez asked when he checked his email again after a cup of coffee in the hotel lobby café:

"If I ever need the extra room, I will have it. Thank you for your help."

Michael said his goodbyes to the hotel staff, and considered taking one last coco taxi to the airport, but instead asked the desk clerk to reserve a more reliable and less adventurous taxi cab for early the following morning. For one final time he walked to *The Escuela Jose' Machado Rodriguez*, appreciating anew the sights and sounds of the street that had become so welcoming and familiar.

Gazing upward through the myriad of telephone and electric wires to the rusty fire escape balconies, he indulged in brief glimpses into private moments of families enjoying meals together. There was a young child dressed only in her underwear; hugging a doll and serving pretend tea. A little boy rolled a truck to an imaginary fire, a toddler in an old crib sucked on a baby bottle with precious little inside. There were puppies nipping and chickens extending wings to claim territory while a teenager banged a pot against a railing as he called obscenities to two young girls as they passed, arm-in-arm. The girls smiled at Michael then flashed a gesture to the boy above their heads. He returned an obscene gesture as if they cared, and went back inside. The girls reminded Michael of Gleynis and Marisol. People laughed and shouted as dominoes clacked. Somewhere a woman was crying. Pigeons cooed from a rafter here, a turret there. And yes, more than one Madonna wept from a cathedral wall.

He walked into *Moorings* and gave his leftover trip money to Denis, almost three thousand dollars in total, so that if he were unable to carry out his plan, Denis would be able to send money to Gleynis and Andre' in Cuba, even if it were a little at a time.

"It'll cost a lot of money to get Gleynis and Andre' out of Cuba once and for all," Michael told Denis as he was sipping a Buccanero at *Moorings* in mid-April.

"That's true, Michael, and unless Gleynis was married to someone from anywhere but Cuba, I'm afraid even with all the money in the world, it would be next to impossible to get her out of there. By the way, here's the address of the doctor that you had inquired about."

"Thank you . . . ." Michael's voice trailed off, his gaze turning toward the harbor where the lights of a cruise ship were shimmering just beyond the twelve-mile limit. Denis and Michael shook hands as Michael left *Moorings* in the early hours of the morning, just as they had done many pleasurable times in the past. The band was playing Bryan Hyland's American hit, "Sealed with a Kiss". The strains of the music connected with Michael as he reached for the door. He turned . .

.

"Denis, that song . . ."

"Si, a crowd pleaser from the summer of 1962 . . ."

The friends nodded to each other and Michael left. Denis stood watching through the window as Michael walked away. He forgot to ask his friend how things went with The Charm of the Heart. Picking up a bar towel Denis began wiping down tables, deliberately skipping the table where a young Puerto Rican couple were sitting close, holding hands, their fingers entwined. Touching each other gently as lovers will, they swayed slowly to the romantic music. The proprietor of *Moorings* watched the couple out of the corner of his eye as the woman handed the man a piece of jewelry: an identification bracelet, a keepsake to be worn on his wrist:

"M-I-G-U-E-L," she spoke the letters as she pointed to each one of them. The man fastened the trinket to his wrist, secured the clasp, and kissed the woman softly on her mouth. The woman and the man's eyes were open, and they looked at each other without speaking after their lips parted. Their attention turned back to the music. Gazing in the direction of the band, they did not see the musicians. The lovers were no longer in Moorings, but far away, in a childhood place where love was new . . . .

" . . . *I'll hear your voice everywhere . . . I'll run to tenderly hold you . . .*"

The music played on. Drawn by the strains of the romantic tune, the woman moved closer to her man. It was her turn to kiss his lips, sealing her devotion; for then, for now, for always . . . .

"Abrázame, mi amor por siempre" she whispered to him as she cuddled until there was no room between them.

Five: Lillian and Gleynis

In an interview some time later, Lillian remembered:

"The telephone rang, waking me up on the third or fourth ring. My caller i. d. read, 'San Juan', but it was not my father's phone number."

Lillian and her brothers returned to San Juan one year later, this time in April. They were there to commit Michael's ashes to sea, and as the small boat, *The Willow*, slowly circled in calm waters a few hundred yards off shore, Lillian read Michael's favorite piece of poetry from "El Viaje Definitivo", The Definitive Journey, by Juan Ramon Jimenez:

... and I will leave. But the birds will stay, singing:

And my garden will stay, with its green tree, with its water well.

Many afternoons the skies will be blue and placid, and the bells in the belfry will chime, as they are chiming this very afternoon. The people who have loved me will pass away, and the town will burst anew every year. But my spirit will always wander nostalgic in the same recondite corner of my flowery garden.

Visibly pregnant, Gleynis recited the selection in Spanish, and as she did, each member of the funeral party scattered a handful of ashes over the placid blue- green water. Lillian told me later she thought that she had heard a peacock call, but realized it was only the creaking and clanging of the anchor rope as the vessel pitched and yawed in the surf. She also told me she thought she saw a man crossing a footbridge in the pool area of a hotel as she set her gaze to the shoreline, but Gleynis reminded her that from where Lillian was standing she was miles away from any hotel.

In the week that the Levi family was in Puerto Rico, bonds were established between Michael's children, his young widow and me. As members of Michael Levi's family, my mother and I were finally permitted to leave Cuba and live in Puerto Rico. If we wished, we were even free to continue on to the United States. Uncle Denis told us we had cousins in Miami, New York, and New Jersey. My mother told her brother, "This is as far as Michael got. This is where we will live, for now . . . ."

". . . and now we will see who will be the first doctor in the family, Andre', *hijo*," my mother said to me the winter before when our paperwork was complete. At first I thought she was only saying that because that is how mothers talk. Then I thought for sure we both believed it could come true. Our schooling, I mean. One thing about me she was wrong about: I think being a lawyer is more to my liking.

Michael had been diagnosed with Hodgkin's disease shortly after returning from Cuba to Puerto Rico, and there was little the doctors could do for him. Any treatment that was available and offered, he refused. My mother and Lillian convinced him to register with a local

195

hospice so that he would be as comfortable as possible in those last days in March. The nurses and counselors coached my mother and Uncle Denis, each with their own role to play as Michael's life slipped away. He died on a damp, cloudy Easter morning that April, in the bedroom of his condominium in San Juan. In the room at the time were my mother and Lillian. Jack and Dashell would arrive late the following day. I had already been sent away for the day to stay with Michael's friend, Professor Robles.

I overheard my mother tell Lillian about a conversation she had had once, at a gathering of friends at Mooring's that evening,

"Michael, it is no use pursuing our relationship any further because, as my grandmother told me when I was a little girl, 'my child, a thousand years will not be enough when you find the one that you will spend your life with'." My mother also told Lillian that she thought she knew Michael as well as anyone could. In him she had discovered the man that her grandmother had described to her; a man for whom she cared for very deeply:

"Hija a mio, mil anos no van a ser suficientes cuando tu encuentres la persona con quien tu vas a compartir el res to de tu vida."

I noticed then that my mother's facial expression changed.

"Did the baby move?" Lillian asked.

"The baby moved."

"Would you like to sit down?"

"It was nothing, but perhaps, yes, perhaps I better . . ."

Andre's San Juan Journal:

Lillian gave me a special gift on that day; The Charm of the Heart. She told me it was special because it came all the way from my great-grandmother Abuela Gutierrez, and even before that. Lillian said that it would bring good luck. I showed the charm to my Uncle Denis the next day. He smiled and agreed that it was indeed lucky that the Charm of the Heart came back to the family. Later that day Denis told me all about The Charm and that its rightful owner was his brother Enrique'. He said, "Andre', if you ever find yourself in Havana, it would be a good idea to look up your Uncle Enrique' and return The Charm to him.

"Well, Uncle, there is no chance of that," I said.

"We'll see," my Uncle answered.

Lillian returned to the United States with her father's remaining journals. These contained the final year of Michael's written work, up until he had grown too weak to lift his pen. Gleynis gave Jack and Dashell their father's personal belongings: his jewelry box containing various objects he'd collected throughout his life, some books, and his musical instruments.

"Lillian, your father told me you are considering becoming a writer."

"I already am a writer, Gleynis."

"What I wanted to say to you is they have an excellent graduate program here at the University, and I could use a roommate."

"Is that so? Thank you. I'll think about it. What do you hear from Marisol?"

"I'm sure she's fine. Marisol's a survivor. The times are changing, Lillian. Fidel is as good as out, and his brother Raul is not getting any younger. They belong to an old way of thinking. Worked for a few then, but not any more, you know? You, too, have a new president. Maybe we'll find Marisol here in Puerto Rico one day soon."

Two years after Michael's death Lillian would write in the dedication of her first novel, Sealed with a Kiss: A Caribbean Journey:

"My father told me once that time was a tricky treasure. He showed me by his example how to make the most out of the short time that we have in this world."

Lillian included in her work a piece of writing that she had finished for her father; an item that she first discovered as a torn journal entry given to her by Denis in his restaurant the first time the two had met: The Man with the Butterfly Tattoo and the Angel Who Loved Him

Part II

By Michael James and Lillian Levi

. . . and if the lovers were ever in the same stadium,

The same shopping mall, or the same church,

They never knew it, for

Their paths never crossed again.

Just as the butterfly is not meant for the net,

198

Nor intended to be on display for the world to see,

The lovers' embrace is a fleeting glimpse,

A hint of what one day may come to be.

Andre's San Juan journal:

What are my plans? I haven't decided what I am going to do with my life. I know one thing, though: After I complete my degree I'd like to return to Cuba; Maybe I'll find my Uncle Enrique'. I owe Uncle Denis that much.

My mother . . . ? No one can say what's inside another heart, but the people of Cuba can always use one good doctor who will not leave them.

Andre' Gutierrez Rodriguez (Levi)

San Juan, Puerto Rico

April 2014

End

Acknowledgements

Thanks to: Brenda Arnowitz, Sam Arnowitz, Ethan Arnowitz, Emma Arnowitz, Randy Arnowitz, Paul Goldblatt, Dave Bluestein, Fred Baylor, and Boe.

In memory of: Lonni Arnowitz and Loren Brooke Osmun

Hermanas hasta el fin del mundo.

Made in the USA
Charleston, SC
26 November 2010